Finding
APEMAN

M.G. HIGGINS

NORTHERN PLAINS
PUBLIC LIBRARY
Ault, Colorado

SADDLEBACK
EDUCATIONAL PUBLISHING

GRAVEL ROAD

Bi-Normal
Edge of Ready
Falling Out of Place
Finding Apeman *(rural)*
A Heart Like Ringo
  Starr *(verse)*
I'm Just Me
Otherwise *(verse)*
Rodeo Princess *(rural)*

Screaming Quietly
Self. Destructed.
Skinhead Birdy
Teeny Little Grief
  Machines *(verse)*
2 Days
Unchained
Varsity 170

SADDLEBACK
EDUCATIONAL PUBLISHING
www.sdlback.com

ISBN-13: 978-1-68021-062-0
ISBN-10: 1-68021-062-9
eBook: 978-1-63078-378-5

Printed in Guangzhou, China
NOR/0615/CA21500932

19 18 17 16 15   1 2 3 4 5

CHAPTER 1

Convoy's house reeks. I could get high just standing in his living room. I look around while he's filling my order. Hundreds of plants on makeshift sawhorse tables. Grow lights. Fans. Classic hard rock thumping in the background.

I've been here a few times. It's still impressive. He's got an outside grow too, hidden under the redwood trees. Or so he tells me. The location is secret. He doesn't want people ripping him off.

"Here you go." Convoy emerges from a bedroom. He hands me a paper sack. With his long beard, fat belly, and overalls, he looks like Santa Claus. Or maybe Santa Claus's grungy brother.

"Thanks." I take it from him.

"Almost trimming season," he says. "Want a job?"

"Maybe." My friend Eric told me trimming pays good, but it's tedious. And I'm always worried about getting busted. There's a California medical certificate tacked to Convoy's living room wall. This is clearly more than what's legal. I'm nervous. "So, see ya," I say. Then I head to the door.

"Hey, Diego," he says. "Got a minute?"

"Not really."

"Come on. I want to show you something. You'll appreciate this."

I take a breath. I want to leave. But I'm curious enough to say, "Okay. A minute."

I follow Convoy's wide butt down a long hallway. Turn to the right. He stops in a small room pasted on the back of the house. That's typical for the old houses around here. Lots of add-ons. What's not so typical is what's in the room. Beakers. Bunsen burners. Scales. Chemicals. I glue myself in the doorway. Don't want to get any closer.

"What is it?" I ask, although I have a good idea.

"Meth." Convoy grins. "I'm branching out."

"Is it safe?" The lab looks sloppy to me. Like it could blow up any second.

He shrugs. "It's safe if you know what you're doing."

"Don't you make enough money with weed?"

"There's never enough, son. I'm supporting an ex-wife and four kids. Anyway, how much more trouble can I get into?"

He has a point. But now I'm even more nervous. "I have to go."

"I've got some ready," he says. "Nice quality." He pulls

two tiny bags from his pocket. White powder sparkles inside. "Try it. Give one away. Let me know what you think about it."

"No thanks."

"Are you sure? It will sell itself."

"Yeah, I know. I'm just ... I'm not into it," I say.

He shrugs. "Suit yourself."

I'm out of there. Convoy's pit bull and Rottweiler follow me down the front steps. I forget their names. I'd pet them, but I haven't figure out if they're friendly or just pretending. I shove the bag of weed into my backpack. Ride my bike down Convoy's gravel driveway to the dirt road.

It rained this morning. The road is muddy and slick. Redwood trees tower over me, filtering out the sunlight. It takes all of my focus not to slide and take a header.

A mile later I reach the paved highway. The emerald forest turns into pastures. I ride past dairy farms. Sheep farms. Goat farms. The cheese factory where my aunt works. Into the town of Seton, where cows, sheep, and goats way outnumber people.

I park my bike next to our duplex. Lock it to the gas meter. I want to keep the bike in my room, but my aunt births a cow (heh) when I get mud in the house.

I head straight to my room. Rummage in the corner of my closet. Toss shoes and my soccer ball off the old wooden toy box. Slide it across the floor. Pull the sandwich bags and scale out from under a stuffed tiger and an old Xbox. Convoy bought the scale for me. After I explained my aunt and dad would not understand why a seventeen-year-old needed a scale.

I set a clean sheet of drawing paper on the floor. Carefully measure out several one-ounce bags. I like this part. It's like a meditation. Weigh weed. Seal weed in sandwich bags. Layer bags in toy box. It gives me time to think. Not always a good thing. But I do it anyway.

I think about Convoy and his new meth lab. Seems like a risk, but what do I know? He's right. He's already in major trouble if he gets busted. He's also right about meth selling itself. Lots of kids at school use it. Adults too. People who buy my weed often ask if I can get meth for them.

But no. No way. I'm afraid I'd like it. Get hooked. Anyway, I don't need a lot of money. Just enough to support my weed habit. Buy a few art supplies. Save for tuition to art school.

My phone dings. It's a text from Tanya. "U home? I'm alone XOXO <3"

I text back, "Cool. See u in a few"

My task done, I set aside two bags. One for me, one for Tanya. I put the remaining weed and scale in the bottom of the toy box. Put the toys back inside. And return the box to the closet. Layer the shoes and ball on top. Close the door.

Shake the scraps of weed from the drawing paper onto joint paper. Add more from my baggie. Roll it. Stick it in my pocket.

I walk down the block to Tanya's apartment. Give her a freebie bag. Sit on her bed. Smoke the joint. Get blissfully high. Listen to a new song she downloaded. Talk about stuff. Laugh. Eat pork rinds, the only snack food in her family's kitchen.

I sketch Tanya's portrait on the inside cover of her notebook. I love how her dark brown hair curves in this perfect arc around her cheek and under her chin. And she gets this pouty look that's sexy and evil and innocent, all at the same time. I hold the drawing up for her when I'm finished. "What do you think?"

She stares at it. "You made me into a cartoon."

"Well, yeah, what else? But it's a good cartoon, right?"

She takes the notebook from me. Studies it. Slowly smiles. "It's awesome. I look like Cat Woman. Or Batgirl. I'm fierce!"

Fierce. That's it. I lean my head against the wall. Take a deep breath. Life is good.

Then I make the mistake of telling her about Convoy's meth lab. Her eyes grow wide. "He'll start you off for free," she says. "Can you get me some?"

Then we argue. And life isn't so good.

I walk home, my high wearing off.

CHAPTER 2

My aunt's in the kitchen when I step through the back door. "What's for dinner?" I ask. I'm starving. Pork rinds only go so far. I look in the pots on the stove.

"Get your nose out of there," she says in her thick Spanish accent. She threatens me with a wooden spoon. "Spaghetti."

"Spaghetti! Awesome."

She eyes me. Guess my enthusiasm was over-the-top.

"Did you weed the front yard like I asked?" she says.

Weed. I laugh.

"What is wrong with you, Diego?"

"Nothing. Sorry. No, I did not *weed.* I'll do it tomorrow."

"So what did you do all day?" she asks.

I pause. "Homework. Went to Tanya's."

"You need to get more exercise. Whatever happened to that soccer club?"

"Tobias dropped out. Then there weren't enough members. Coach Nickel wanted to quit anyway."

She turns back to the stove. Stirs.

"I rode my bike today," I tell her.

"Saints be praised."

The front door opens and closes. "I'm home!"

Dad! I trot to the living room. "I didn't know you'd be home today."

We hug. He pats my back. "Job ended early." His accent is as thick as my aunt's. It would be easier for them to speak Spanish. But I was born in the U.S. They've always spoken English. They want me to fit in. The only Spanish I've learned from them is *tía* (aunt). Everything else I've learned in Spanish class at school. White kids can't believe I'm not acing that class.

"How long till you go out again?" I ask.

"A few days."

Dad works as a labor foreman. He goes wherever crops need picking. Farmers hire Dad to tell workers what to do. Something's always ripening in California. So he's always away from home. It's March now. Asparagus and avocado season.

"Long drive from Sacramento." He presses his back and winces. "When's dinner?"

"Ten minutes!" Tía calls from the kitchen.

"Good," he says. "Then I'm going to bed." He must see the disappointed look on my face. It would be fine if he was a jerk and I hated him. But I happen to like my dad. I wish he were home more. "It's Saturday," he says. "I thought you'd have a million things to do."

I do. But if he'll only be here a few days, I'd rather stay home. "We could watch some TV," I say.

He smiles. Pats my arm. "I would just go to sleep."

He does look tired. Probably started driving at dawn. "Well. There is a party in town. I was going to take Tanya."

"Are you walking?" he asks.

I nod.

"Then go. Have a good time. But be home by midnight and no drinking. Tell Tanya hi for me."

We eat dinner. Dad's an amazing storyteller. He somehow makes working in asparagus fields seem like a big adventure, though I know it's really hard work. If his life had turned out differently, I think he would have been an actor. Or a writer. "How are the studies?" he asks.

Oh man. I'm always afraid he's going to bring this up. I could sure use another hit right now.

"Diego?" he says.

"Fine."

He looks at Tía. She shrugs. "No notes home," she says. "No phone calls from school."

Dad sighs. "I added money to your college fund this week. Have you been exploring schools?"

As a matter of fact, I have. Just not the ones he wants me to go to. "A few," I answer.

"Which ones?"

I drag my fork through the spaghetti sauce on my plate. Make a crosshatch pattern. It looks interesting.

"Diego," Dad says. "Which colleges?"

"California College of the Arts. Art Center. CalArts. A few others." I crosshatch over my crosshatches, making little squares.

"You know I want more for you."

I glance up from my plate. "I know." There's nothing more to say. We're never going to agree on this. I'm not cut out to be a doctor. Or a lawyer. Or an engineer. The things he'd like me to be.

"Well, you're still a junior. You have a little while to decide. So let's not argue." He pushes away from the table. Looks like an old man as he slowly gets to his feet.

I hate disappointing him.

"Thank you for dinner, Marta," he says. "It was delicious. Good night."

"Good night," Tía and I say.

I carry dishes to the kitchen. Then go to my room. Open the toy box. Remove three bags and shove them into my jacket pockets. I'll share one at the party. Sell the other two.

I'll never earn enough money to pay for art school by myself. It's too expensive. I'm hoping by the time I graduate, my father will come around. I'll convince him

I'm doing the right thing. He'll be proud of me. Want to support me.

The Scott twins' party is so-so. The usual kids from school are there. Plus some local stoners. Two bikers crash it, setting everyone on edge. But they settle in. There's a keg, and Chris Hanes brings a bottle of whiskey he stole from home. I follow Dad's directions and don't drink. But I smoke my butt off and pass my weed around. Sell both bags.

Then the hard drugs start showing up on the coffee table. It always happens. That's why I'm sitting on the other side of the room. My arm around Tanya. She makes a move to get up. I hold her.

"Let me go," she says.

"Why? Where are you going?"

"To the bathroom! God, Diego."

I loosen my grip. Watch her traipse down the hall.

"Wow, possessive much?" says her friend Anise. She jumps up to go with Tanya.

I could explain. How Tanya's entire family is addicted to drugs. How Tanya is probably a snort away from the same fate. But why should I? If Anise doesn't know that already, then she's not a very good friend.

One of my joints circles back around. I take a long hit. Man, Convoy grows the best stuff. I lean my head back. Close my eyes. This awesome apeman appears in my mind. Kind of like Big Foot, only he's part robot. A bionic apeman. Swinging through the trees. Shooting the bad guys—evil alien monkeys—with a bionic laser gun built into his arm.

Oh man. I have got to draw this before I forget.

I open my eyes. Wish I'd saved room in my jacket for my sketchbook. Look around for one of the Scotts to ask to borrow a pencil and paper. That's when I see Tanya. Sitting at the coffee table.

CHAPTER 3

Now I wish I wasn't so wasted. I need to be cool about this. Need to say the right thing. Oh, screw it. I need to get her out of here. Now.

Her back is to me. I lean over. Whisper in her ear, "It's time to leave."

She shakes her head. I don't know what she's snorted, if anything.

"Come on." I press my hand on her shoulder.

She shrugs it away. "If you need to leave, then go," she says. "I can find my way home."

I'm not leaving her alone. I kneel behind her. Stroke her arm. "I want you to go with me." I kiss her neck. "Is your house empty?"

She shivers from my touch. Nods.

"Then come on. Let's go."

She pauses a long moment. Then gets to her feet. We walk to her place.

◈

I sit in English class Monday morning. Mr. Dawson is talking about Shakespeare. I'm doodling the bionic apeman. Thankfully I didn't forget about him when I sobered up. Although he's not coming out as awesome as he appeared in my mind Saturday night. Apes aren't all that easy to draw.

I turn the page. Pretend to take notes. Think about yesterday. Spending the day with Dad. We went to church. Kicked the soccer ball around. Drove forty minutes to the hardware store. Got washers to fix the dripping bathroom faucet that was driving Tía nuts. He bought me a burger. Then we came home. Fixed the faucet. Pulled weeds in the front yard. Watched TV. Neither of us once mentioned college. It was a good day.

"Diego?" Mr. Dawson says.

I look at him.

"Wake up," he says. "Your turn."

I look down at the book we're reading aloud. Tanya is sitting next to me. She presses her finger on a passage. I hope that's what I'm supposed to read. I go for it.

"Here is the scroll of every man's name, which is thought fit, through all Athens, to play in our interlude before the duke and the duchess, on his wedding day at night."

In front of me, Becca continues reading without being asked. I follow along for a while. Then I get bored. Shakespeare's not really my thing. Though I bet the comic book version would be awesome. I would definitely read that.

"Okay, that's enough," Mr. Dawson says. "The bell's about to ring. For those of you who love Shakespeare—and I know you all do—you'll be glad to hear this year's school play is *A Midsummer Night's Dream.*"

I think that's the book we're reading. I flip to the cover. Yep.

"I am again serving as director. Tryouts are next Tuesday. Extra credit for participating." He grins. "Be there or be square."

I roll my eyes. The bell rings. I gather my stuff. Walk down the hall with Tanya. Hold her hand.

Matt Unser comes up on my other side. "Hey, Diego," he says. "How's it going?" He slips bills into my palm. I shove them in my pocket. Pull out a bag and give it to him. "Thanks, dude," he says.

"Sure. See ya."

Tanya has been quiet all morning. I texted her a few times yesterday. Her responses were brief. Lacked their usual Xs, Os, and <3s. I think she's still mad I took her away from the party early. I'm not sorry at all. She said she didn't take anything. I'm pretty sure I believe her. We had a nice time at her place. She wasn't hyper or zoned out.

I squeeze her hand. She doesn't squeeze back.

"You should try out for that play," I tell her. "The *Midsummer* whatever. You'd be great at it."

"I can't act."

"Yes you can. You're a natural. You're very emotive."

"I don't know even what that means," she says.

"It means you're good at expressing your feelings. Like right now. That frown. The crease between your eyes. They say you hate me."

"I don't hate you."

"But you're pissed off."

She lets go of my hand. "You're controlling, Diego. You're always telling me what to do."

I think about it. Okay. Yeah, maybe I am controlling. But it's for her own good. "I just want what's best for you."

"How can you possibly know what's best for me? Maybe you need to let me make my own decisions. Even if you think they're mistakes."

We've reached math. This is not the time or place to talk about drugs. About ruining herself. About ruining us. "Let's go to class," I say.

"Fine." She shoves my shoulder as she storms past me.

"Fine."

I sit at my desk. Try to pay attention instead of draw. I can't afford to fail anything. Art schools are competitive. They like well-rounded students. Good GPAs.

But my mind keeps finding its way back to Tanya. I want her to be in the school play so she has something to do. Something to look forward to. She doesn't play sports. Doesn't have a job. Doesn't care about school. Doesn't care about much of anything. It makes me sad. I think I'm the only person who gives a frig about what happens to her.

I'm bionic apeman. Swooping through the jungle. Grabbing apegirl by the waist. Yanking her from the clutches of the evil alien monkeys. Then we have an ape-baby and live happily ever after. In an awesome three-story tree house. That I design myself. It even has a hot tub.

CHAPTER 4

Last period. Electives. For me, that's art. I like saving the best for last. Although our teacher, Ms. Evans, isn't all that hyped on art. Our school is small, and she's also the girls' gym teacher and soccer coach. There's a big soccer tournament coming up. She's busy.

I'm already at my table. Working on Apeman. (Yes, now with a capital *A*.) Other students wander in. Tanya's elective is music appreciation. I guess it's good we don't share every class together. She seems to need her space.

My friend Eric sits next to me. "How's it going?" he asks.

"Okay."

"Did you go to the twins' party?"

"Yeah. You didn't miss anything."

"Really? I heard it got gnarly. A biker dude and Jimmy got into a rip-roaring fight. Cops came," he says.

"Tanya and I left early."

"Good thing, I guess."

"Yeah. Good thing." The last thing I need is to get searched and arrested. Crap.

The bell rings. Ms. Evans trots into the classroom five minutes late. She's wearing workout clothes. She always wears workout clothes. They're all the same style. Just different colors. This one is tangerine.

"Sorry I'm late," she says. "I want you to do the same assignment as yesterday. Create one drawing or painting. Use at least three techniques you've learned over the semester. Shading, perspective, contrast, proportion, negative space. You know the drill."

I almost expect her to order us to do a few sit-ups before we start.

Kids start getting out their art supplies. I focus on Apeman.

"Diego, can I talk to you for a second?"

I look up. Ms. Evans's eyes are locked on mine. What did I do? I step slowly to the front of the class.

"I've got a soccer emergency," she whispers. "It will take me about twenty minutes to deal with it. Can you watch the class while I'm gone?"

"Watch it. What do you mean?"

"Just make sure no one steals anything. Throws things. Gets in a fight." She raises her eyebrows. Talk about emoting. She's desperate.

I shrug. "Okay. Sure."

"Thank you." She runs out.

I stand in the front of the classroom. Feel a rush of power. She chose me. Me. Over every other student. And there are some definite suck-ups in here. Lisa Cogsworth. Kelly Myers. John West. All straight-A students. The thing is, they're taking art just for the credits. I'm taking it because, well … because I'm an artist.

"Anybody need help?" I ask. "Have any questions about the assignment?"

A wad of paper hits me in the face. "Sit down," Eric says.

I point two fingers at my eyes and then at him. "I'm watching you, man. Don't make me send you to the principal's office."

"Asswipe." Good thing he says it with a smile.

I sit and do my work. Ms. Evans returns fifteen minutes later. She glances at me. Mouths, *Thank you.* I nod. So ends my fifteen minutes of teaching fame.

I meet Tanya after sixth period. "Ms. Evans had to leave class today. Guess who she left in charge?"

"Must have been you or you wouldn't be asking."

"That's right. Think I'll tell my dad. Better yet, maybe I'll ask her to write a letter. She can tell him what an asset I am to her class. A leader. That he should send me to art school. Or the world will miss out."

"On your comic books?"

I shrug. "Nothing wrong with comic books. They've inspired generations of Americans."

She's quiet.

"What's up?" I ask.

"Nothing. I was just thinking about the play. Wondering if I should try out."

"Of course you should try out. That would be awesome!" I say.

"But I don't know if I can do it. I'll have to memorize lines."

"It can't be that hard. I'll help."

"I'm afraid of making a fool of myself. Remember the third grade play on oral hygiene?" she says. "I had my lines memorized. Then I saw Mom in the audience and freaked out. Mrs. Sullivan had to prompt me. Mom said I barely spoke above a whisper. I thought I was shouting."

"So? That was then. You're not a shy eight-year-old girl anymore."

We've reached our lockers. She throws all her books inside. She's about to close it. I hold it open. Grab *A Midsummer Night's Dream*. Hand it to her. "I believe in you, Tanya."

She reluctantly takes the book. "I was thinking," she says as she waits for me to open my locker. "Don't plays have sets?"

"Sure. I guess."

"Maybe you could make them."

I stare at her. "I don't know how to make sets."

She shrugs. "I don't know how to act."

"But that's different."

"How?" she asks.

"How?" I sputter. "Uh, gee. There's construction involved. Building big things. Wood. Tools. And painting. I don't build and I don't paint." I shake my head. "I make drawings, Tanya. Little drawings. With pencils and paper."

"Okay. Whatever. Don't challenge yourself." She turns and walks away.

I catch up to her. We leave the building and head home. I don't know what to say. I feel like a dweeb. But I can't make sets for a play. It's beyond my abilities. I need to smoke. "Can I come over?"

"Mom's home today. And Henry has been hanging around." Her mom is a maid at the motel up the highway. Henry is her mom's latest loser boyfriend. "What about your place?" she asks.

"Can't. Dad's home."

We walk quietly for a while. "Did you hear Steph's having a party on Friday?" Tanya asks.

"No." I kick a rock up the dirt path.

"I'd like to go."

"Okay. Nothing else to do." I'm not looking forward to

herding her away from coffee tables all night. But it will give me a chance to sell more weed.

We reach her apartment building. Kiss. Separate.

I wish she hadn't mentioned the sets for the play. Now I feel like an ass. Like I chickened out or something. Even though that's not how it is.

Dad's not home. Thank God. I open my window a crack. Get nicely baked.

CHAPTER 5

A couple of days pass. I come home Thursday afternoon. Dad's truck is in the driveway. Shoot. I won't be able to smoke. I think about backtracking. Slipping behind the church, one of my alternate spots. But he's leaving for a job tomorrow. Maybe I should stay straight.

I walk in the front door. "Dad?" He's not in the living room. Or the kitchen. I grab a bag of corn chips and head to my room.

He's standing in my room. His back to me. The closet door is open. His head is lowered. He's looking at something.

My heart freezes. He's found my stash. He will kill me. Or have me arrested. Or both. I have excuses stored in my head. But they're all lame. He won't believe me.

He must hear my frozen heart clink because he turns. His eyes narrow, pissed off. "Diego," he says.

"Hi, Dad," I say lightly. "What's up?"

Then I remember I left my closet open this morning. And I don't see the toy box anywhere. He reaches for my desk. Picks up one of my sketchbooks. "You've been doing a lot of drawing."

Oh. My heart starts beating again, but slowly. "Yeah. So?"

He sets the sketchbook down. Paws through a few more. "How much time do you spend on this?"

"Hard to say."

"You should spend the time studying," he says.

"I study."

"Enough? You're grades should be better."

I force myself not to roll my eyes. "Dad. I don't want to be a doctor."

"You don't have to be a doctor. But there's no future in this." He points at my drawings.

"Yes there is. Companies hire people to draw comic books. They hire graphic designers. There are lots of jobs I can do as an artist." I think about art class the other day. "I could even teach."

His shoulders rise and fall as he takes a deep breath. "I want you to be successful. I don't want you to struggle."

"Well, that's what going to art school is about, right? I get good grades. Put a portfolio together. Get a degree. A company hires me. This isn't the crapshoot you think it is, Dad. I've done my research."

He shakes his head. He's not getting it. He's not connecting the dots between my little drawings and a real career. "Anyway, I can do more than draw. There's a school play. I'm thinking of making the sets. They're going to be awesome. Incredible." I immediately want to shove the words back in my mouth. I am such an idiot.

He nods. "I'll look forward to seeing them." He leaves my room.

I sit on my bed. My hands shake. I need to smoke. I jump up. Open my sock drawer. Shake the pipe from a sock. "I'll be back in a few!" I'm out the door. Go to the church. They're having a meeting. Lots of people milling around. I jump on my bike. Head to the woods, my second alternate spot.

It's damp. Dark. Secluded. No houses in view. I don't know if this land is private or public. Doesn't matter. As long as no one comes after me with a shotgun.

I sit on the ground. Light up. Take a few good puffs. Feel calmer. I could live here in the forest. Pitch a tent. Gaze all day at the light filtering through the redwoods. A lot of people do exactly that. These woods are full of homeless people. Crazy people. I guess there are worse places to survive.

Why did I tell Dad I was making those sets? I just totally screwed myself. I don't even know if Mr. Dawson will let me. Guess I can ask. Make an effort. If I remember right, a lot of the play takes place outdoors. In the woods. Like the scene I'm looking at right now. A small opening in the forest. Lots of ferns.

The school play from a couple years ago had sets. So I know generally what they look like. I start thinking it out in my head. One or two trees on each side of the stage. A painted backdrop with more trees. Kind of fantastical. Ms. Evans might let me work on it during sixth period. Since I'm her star pupil and everything.

I bike home. Keep thinking about it. The more I plan, the more excited I get. I even forget Dad's disappointment. His disapproval. Because once he sees what I've done, he'll be like, "My son is awesome! Get this kid to art school, pronto!" Not that my dad would say awesome or anything.

Tía eyes me when I walk in the back door. "Where have you been?"

"Biking. I, uh, needed the exercise."

She loses her scowl. "Well, all right. It's almost time for dinner. Wash up. And set the table."

I'm washing my hands at the kitchen sink when the phone rings. Tía answers it.

"Hello." Pause. "Yes." Pause. "Yes." There's a super-long pause. I'm almost done setting the table when she says, "I see." She grabs a pen and writes something on the pad next to the phone. "We'll call you back." Pause. "Soon." Pause. "Yes, I understand. Goodbye."

She stands there. Stares at the phone. Spaced out.

"Tía?" I ask. "Who was that?"

"People from the government. Refugee Resettlement. Your cousins from Guatemala are in Arizona."

I try to process what she just said. Can't. "What cousins from Guatemala?"

She steps into the living room. Talks to Dad. I can't remember the last time I heard them speak Spanish to each other. This does not bode well.

CHAPTER 6

I catch bits and pieces of Dad and Tía's conversation. *Madre. Padre. Norte.* Basic words that don't help me figure out what's going on.

My family is from Guatemala. I know that much. Dad and Mom crossed the US–Mexican border in the 1990s. Civil war in Central America made normal life pretty much impossible there. They ended up at a chicken processing plant in California's Central Valley.

That's where Mom died. Dad never gave me the details. It was an industrial accident of some sort. The plant's fault. But my parents were illegal. Expendable. Dad didn't dare take the company to court. To this day he doesn't eat chicken—from that company or any other.

I was born here. I was two when Mom died. Dad couldn't work and also raise me. So his sister, Marta—Tía—came north to help out. It's been the three of us ever since. I think Tía and Dad have a younger brother. They don't talk about family much. I don't ask.

As far as I'm concerned, I'm American. I think Dad and Tía have been happy to keep it that way.

I'm standing in the doorway between the kitchen and living room. My arms crossed. Waiting for them to finish talking. Their faces and gestures are intense. But they're not arguing. It's more like they're trying to figure something out. Finally Dad says, "*Sí, sí. Claro.*" He faces me. Waves me into the room.

I keep my arms crossed. Don't think I'm going to like what he tells me.

"Your two cousins, Arturo and Carlos, are in the United States," he says, "They traveled through Mexico to Texas. They turned themselves in to immigration when they arrived."

"What? Why?"

"Same old story. Upheaval in Guatemala." Dad gets a disgusted look on his face. "Only now it's drug gangs. They're forcing young men to join them. And if the children don't join, the gangs kill them. Our brother wrote my name and Marta's on a piece of paper. And our phone number. He sent his boys north. The situation must be desperate, or he never would have done this."

"Carlos is fourteen. Arturo is ten," Tía says. "They have nowhere else to go. So they'll stay with us."

"What?"

"It will be a challenge," Dad says. "But we'll cope.

We're the boys' only relatives in America. If we don't take them, they'll likely be sent back to Guatemala. We must help them."

No we mustn't, I want to say. "If you haven't noticed, all of our bedrooms are taken. Where will they sleep?"

Dad thinks. Shrugs. "With you. I still have to leave tomorrow. This job will last a couple of weeks. You and Tía arrange your room. Buy whatever furniture you need."

My jaw has dropped. "Do I get any say in this?"

Dad's eyes narrow. "My son is not so heartless."

Uh, yeah, I am. When it comes to my room. But he's obviously not going to budge. So I guess I have no choice. "Okay. Fine."

"You don't know how good you have it, Diego."

"I said fine! When will my long-lost cousins be here?"

"A couple of weeks," Tía says. "They're at an immigration facility. They'll arrive by bus."

Oh joy.

"Dinner's ready," she says.

We eat quietly. From their vacant stares, I get the feeling they're lost in thought. Maybe remembering their pasts. The people they left behind. Okay, I'm a dickwad. I don't know what my cousins have gone through to get across the border.

I need to suck it up. This isn't the end of the world. A comet isn't barreling toward Northern California. A scourge of evil alien monkeys hasn't landed in our backyard. Though that might be kind of cool.

I suddenly remember the sets for the school play. Crap. My cousins. School. One of them is fourteen? That means he'll be going to high school with me. Does he even speak English? Crappity-crap-crap. I've got enough going on. What about my weed business?

I take a deep breath. *Suck it up, Diego. Suck it up.*

I go to my room after dinner. Send Tanya a really long text. Explain what's going on.

She texts back, "Wow."

That's it. *Wow.* Well, what else can she say? I'm very sorry for the pending upheaval in your life and wish you well.

Then she sends another text, "We still going to Steph's party?"

I respond in the affirmative. Then I grab a sketchbook. Draw my ideas for the sets. That way I'll have something to show Mr. Dawson. I have two weeks before my life changes. In the meantime, I'll focus on things I have control of—like my future career.

Dad and I say our goodbyes later that night. He gives me a hug. Pats my back. "You're a good boy. Thank you for doing right by your cousins." He's gone Friday morning before I'm awake.

ᗡ

I stay late after English the next day. Mr. Dawson is erasing the whiteboard. "Uh, Mister Dawson?"

He looks over. Sees it's me. Keeps erasing. "What's up, Diego?"

"I've been thinking about the play."

"Tryouts are next Tuesday," he says.

"I don't want to act. I want to do the sets."

He stops erasing.

"See?" I show him my sketchbook. "A redwood forest. Thought it might be interesting to make it local."

He steps over. Takes a look. "Nice." Then he shakes his head. "But no. That's too elaborate."

"Not really. I can do it."

"Have you ever made sets before?" he asks.

"No."

"There are only six weeks before the play. What you're showing me will take a lot of work. And money. The budget is zero. I was planning on bringing a couple potted plants from home. Use some risers for the interior scenes."

"That's lame," I say.

"The important thing is the acting, Diego. The words themselves. That's what the audience will pay attention to."

I tuck the book under my arm. "Not me. I'm visual. An awesome set will make the play awesome. A lame set will make the play lame."

He sighs. Taps the eraser against his leg. Realizes he's getting marker dust on his pants. "Shoot." He brushes it off

"So can I?" I ask.

"I don't know. I'd want a teacher to supervise you. I don't have the time."

"Ms. Evans might."

"Can you raise your own money for supplies?" he asks.

"I think so."

He seems to think about it. "Fine. I'll pitch in fifty dollars."

"Great."

"Be prepared to modify your plans, though. Simple is okay. And keep your receipts. I'll want to see them."

"Okay. Thanks. You won't regret this." I head out of the classroom.

"Diego?" he calls. "I'll give you extra credit. Like I'm giving the actors. Seems only fair."

"Awesome."

One more hurdle to go, and I'm on my way to set-making stardom.

CHAPTER 7

Ms. Evans holds my sketchbook after class. Studies my drawing for the set. I thought she'd be a pushover. But she looks as doubtful as Mr. Dawson.

"Where will you do the work?" she asks.

Hmm. Good question. "Here?"

She shakes her head. "Not enough room. I think your only choice is the backstage of the auditorium. You'd have to get that okayed by Principal Wright."

My shoulders slump.

"You're planning to make the trees from plywood?" she asks.

"Yeah."

"Do you have power tools? Do you know how to use them? What kind of wood will you use?" She must see the dazed look on my face. "I'm sorry, Diego. But you need to plan. Figure things out ahead of time."

"Sure. I know."

"Why don't you come up with a list? Include all the materials you'll need. Supplies. Tools. Get the okay from Principal Wright. Then I'll supervise you," she says.

"Okay."

"And you might want to recruit some other students to help." She hands the sketchbook back to me.

I leave the classroom. Tanya meets me outside. I rip out the drawing. Chuck it in a trash can.

"What are you doing?" she asks.

"Too much work. Screw it."

"Diego." She pulls the page from the trash. "What will your dad say if you don't even try?"

"Low blow." I take it from her.

We pass the office. I think about stopping. Talking to Mrs. Wright. But she's not one of my biggest fans. And I'm not one of hers. I'll do it next week.

᪣

Tía comes to my room when she gets home. Sniffs. "What's that smell?"

Shoot. I smoked longer than usual. Coping with my crappy day. Guess my room didn't air out enough. "I don't smell anything," I say.

Her eyes narrow. "Is that marijuana?"

"No! Of course not. Tanya got me a new cologne. It's … different."

She crosses her arms. I don't think she's buying it. But she must not want to argue because she says, "We need to talk about your room."

"Okay."

She looks around. "It's not big enough for two beds. So a bunk bed. Where do you want it to go?"

"In the hallway," I say.

"Diego."

I sigh. "Over there, I guess." I point to the wall across the room, near the door. I want my bed to stay where it is. Close to the closet. So I can keep tabs on my toy box.

Tía nods. "We'll go to Walmart tomorrow."

"Walmart. Awesome." The closest Walmart store is a two-hour drive. Not my idea of a good time. But I'm the loving cousin. The son with the big heart. "I'm going to a party tonight," I inform her.

She eyes me. "You go to a lot of parties."

"Well, yeah. There's nothing else to do around here."

"You know your father's rules. Be home by midnight and no drinking." Then she says, "I could drive you and Tanya into town sometime. We could all go to the movies."

I pretend like I'm thinking about it. "Sure. I'll ask her."

She pats my cheek. "I know you're going to be a good cousin. It will be like having brothers."

૭

Tanya and I ride with Eric to Steph's house. If we live in

the boonies, then she lives on Mars. Her parents are out of town. She has an older brother who's supposed to be looking after her. Apparently it was his idea to have the party. I am assuming he let her invite her friends so she wouldn't tattle.

I've got my pockets loaded with merchandise. Hope to land some new clients. Need to pay for those play supplies.

There are a ton of cars. We have to park down the road. Hoof it to the house. The place is packed. Big age-range. Music is blasting. I worry for a second their neighbors will call the cops. But I doubt any neighbors live close enough to complain. I immediately get down to business and start smoking. Pass it around. Let Convoy's product speak for itself.

"You want to dance?" Tanya yells over the music. She's drinking something in a short glass. Not beer.

"No!" I shout back. I don't even feel like standing.

She goes off with her friend Anise. I assume to dance. If there's a coffee table with drugs, I don't see it. I feel a moment of panic. An urge to chase after her. Then I tell myself to chill. I'm going to take her advice. Let her be her own chaperone. Not be so controlling. Because you know what? I'm having enough trouble controlling my own life right now.

I wish my mind was full of drawings of Apeman and evil alien monkeys. But its full of sets I'm not capable of building and my disappointed dad and Guatemalan cousins. Crap, this music is giving me a headache.

"Hey." An older guy I don't know taps my shoulder. Probably goes to the community college with Steph's brother. "I hear you're selling," he says in my ear.

I give him a neutral look. Not yes or no. Can't be too careful with strangers.

"You got meth?" he asks.

I shake my head. He walks away.

This happens three more times during the night. I only sell one bag of weed. And that's to Eric, at a discount. What is wrong with these people? I understand how boring it is in Seton. We all need a little excitement. But that's what weed is for. Dependable, mellow weed. Doesn't rot your teeth. Lets you sleep at night.

Eric tries to hit on several girls with no success. He wants to leave. And it's midnight. Past my curfew. I look for Tanya, who I've only seen a few times. I find her in the kitchen. She's talking a mile a minute to some guy. They keep interrupting each other. Like, "No, you don't get it."

"No, *you* don't get it."

"Get what?" I ask.

"Diego!" She hugs me. "Isn't this party amazing? I'm having such a good time."

"That's cool. Except we need to go," I say.

She sways on her feet. Punches my chest. "Why? We just got here!"

Oh my God, she is so hyper. Drunk and hyper. "Eric needs to leave," I say. "What did you take?"

"I knew you'd be like this," she says. "Why do you have to be like this?"

"I'll take her home," the guy says.

"No way, man. She's my girlfriend."

"Let's go," Eric says behind me.

Crap. I don't know what to do. I'm guessing she got hold of some meth or coke. "Tanya's really high," I tell Eric. "I can't force her to leave. She'll go nuts on me."

"So go without her," he says.

I think about it. I'll get into big trouble if I get home much later. But if something happens to Tanya, I'll never forgive myself. "I can't do that," I tell Eric. "We'll find another ride. You go ahead."

"Are you sure?"

"Yeah," he says.

I stay with Tanya the rest of the night. It's early morning when she decides she's finally ready to leave. Steph's brother drives us home. I'm not a happy camper. Especially when we get into an argument. And I find out this isn't the first time she's tweaked.

CHAPTER 8

I'm walking Tanya to her apartment. Steph's brother just dropped us off. The sun is coming up. I need to get home. If Tía knows I'm not there, she'll be furious. Tell Dad. He'll ground me.

Tanya is hanging all over me. Kissing me. "Come inside, okay? Let's mess around."

Part of me wants to. A big part. But I push her away. "No way."

"You're mad at me," she says.

"Yeah, I'm mad. But I don't want to talk about it right now." I open the door for her.

"I'm not an addict! I just use it every once in a while. I like how it makes me feel. Come on. Please come inside. I'll make it worth your while." She traces her finger down my neck and chest.

I take a deep breath. "I can't. I have to go. I'm in enough trouble already."

"You know what, Diego? You're a wimp. A wimpy

pothead. You suck!" She storms inside. Slams the door behind her.

I shove my hands in my pockets. Don't have the energy to think about what she just said. I march home. Quietly open and close the front door. Tiptoe to my room. Thankfully Tía isn't up.

The next thing I know, someone is shaking my arm. "Diego! Wake up."

I mumble something.

"Diego!" More shaking.

I slowly open my ten-ton eyelids. Tía scowls at me. "It's after eleven. We need to leave for Walmart. What time did you get in?"

Good, she doesn't know. "I'm not sure."

She presses her hands on her hips. "Get out of bed."

I don't want to. But she'll stand there until I'm up. I somehow drag my legs over the side of the bed and get dressed.

೪

The drive to Ukiah is mostly quiet. Tía asks me questions about the party. About school. I give her one-word answers. I'm not trying to be rude. I'm exhausted. Distracted. And I keep thinking about Tanya. The fact she's been using her mom's drugs. How did I not know? How did I not see? I'm angry. But I have a hard time blaming her. The drugs are in her apartment all the time. An easy high. She said she's not

41

addicted. I doubt that. Could be why she bugged me to sell Convoy's new product.

Oh, Tanya. I feel so enormously sad. I want to rescue her, but I don't know how.

We buy a wooden bunk bed at Walmart. A cheap dresser. Cheap desk. We load the boxes in the back of the hatchback. Tie it all in with rope.

I spend Sunday putting the furniture together. The building project gives me a chance to dig around the garage. Inventory Dad's tool. He's got a variety of screw-drivers. A cordless drill. I also find a circular saw. Sandpa-per. Most everything I'd need to make sets for the play.

I still have doubts. Still wonder if it's worth the hassle. But then I read the play Sunday night after dinner. Jeez, it's so hard to understand. Why couldn't Shakespeare write in normal English? But I get the basics—romance, jealousy, love triangles. Funny things happening in the woods. Like I told Mr. Dawson, a nice set would add a whole lot. A couple of potted plants? So lame.

I text Eric. Ask if he wants to help. He works at the Seton convenience store after school. But he says he'll try. That's good enough for me. I'm back on it. Anyway, I'd rather think about making sets than ponder the bunk bed looming on the other side of my room. And my tweaking girlfriend.

⌇

On Monday I pick up Tanya like usual. We didn't communicate after the party. So I don't know what to expect. Does she still think I'm a wimpy pothead? Or the loyal boyfriend who stuck by her side when she really needed me? I know my choice.

She says, "Hi." Doesn't try to kiss me.

"Hi." I follow her lead. Don't try to kiss her either. "How's it going?"

We start walking. She shrugs. Looks straight ahead. Okay. Wimpy pothead, I guess. Which, the more I think about it, really pisses me off. "I could have left you at Steph's party. Deserted you. But I didn't."

"Maybe you should have."

"Really? You were mind-numbingly high. With middle-aged guys hitting on you."

"They were college-age. And maybe you *should* have left me," she says.

"Why? Because they have jobs? Money? They can supply your drug habit?"

"It's not like that. I feel stifled, Diego."

"Stifled?"

"Yes. You stifle me."

"Who have you been talking to? You didn't come up with that word by yourself," I say.

"Why? Because I'm too stupid?" She walks ahead of me.

I catch up. "Hey. I'm sorry. You're not stupid."

She's quiet a long time. Then she says, "I went out with one of those guys on Saturday. A guy from the party."

My stomach curls into a tight ball. Slams up into my chest. Drops to my feet. I'm suddenly woozy. Have to stop walking. Tanya looks back at me. Her expression is flat. Nothing. Just … nonexistent. "I'm sorry, Diego," she says. "I should have told you first. But I don't think we should hang out anymore."

"You're breaking up with me?"

She nods. Walks away.

Wow. Okay. Wow. I was expecting a small fight. Then an apology. A make-up kiss.

I don't try to catch up to her. I need to think. I need to get high. The church is nearby. I scoot around the side. It's a spot bordered on three sides by tall, thick shrubs. I light up my pipe. Inhale. Let my head find a nice coasting spot. Let go a little. Not care a little.

Tanya and I were together since seventh grade. Four years. Holy crap. This feels really awful. I'm sinking. Flailing. Drowning. I take a couple more hits. Hide my pipe in my backpack. Fast-walk to school. Don't want to be tardy. Have Mrs. Wright send another note home. I need the principal on my good side if I'm going to make those sets. If I *want* to make those sets. It's quite possible I don't care anymore.

CHAPTER 9

It's open seating in English. I find an empty desk in the back. Away from Tanya. I'm wallowing in my misery. And I'm high. So I'm not paying much attention to Mr. Dawson. But my brain picks up on his reminder for the play tryouts tomorrow.

I wonder if Tanya's still going. I hope so. Even if she messed around behind my back, and broke up with me, and I'm friggin' angry, I still care about her. Want her to find something good to do with her life.

The bell rings. I jump up. Want to ask if she's going to audition. But she's already heading down the hallway with Anise.

"What's up?" Eric asks. "Why didn't you sit with Tanya today?"

"We, uh." How do I get the words out? "She broke up with me. She went out with some guy from Steph's party."

"Crap. That sucks."

"No kidding."

"But honestly, dude? I think you're better off."

I glare at him. "Like you should know. The guy who's never had a girlfriend."

"Sorry. I'm just sayin'. Her family's a bunch of losers. She would have eventually brought you down too. Want to get high?"

"No thanks. I already am."

The rest of the day is boring. Hollow. So is the rest of the week. I get high. Go to school. Avoid Tanya. Get high. Hang out with Eric, even though he pissed me off about being better off without Tanya. Go home. Get high. Do just enough homework to pass. Try to draw. But my imagination has dried up.

I text Tanya a couple of times. I hope maybe she's changed her mind. Misses me. Wants to get back together. But she doesn't respond. So, yeah. Whatever.

If she auditioned for the play, she didn't get a part. Mr. Dawson posts the results on Thursday. Eric and I study the list. "Hey, what about those sets?" he says. "I thought you needed my help."

"It's on hold. I'll let you know," I say.

"Okay. Cool. Hey, I don't have to work this afternoon. Want to come over?"

"And do what?" I ask.

He shrugs. "Watch Netflix. Play a video game. Kick a ball around."

"Sure. Fine."

I walk home. Hear Spanish filter though the windows.

Oh, crap. Are they here already? I thought I had another week before *Cousinaggedon.* I cannot handle this. I turn around. Head for Eric's.

"Diego!" Tía opens the front door. Waves me over. "Come meet your cousins." She's got a big maternal smile on her face.

I trudge slowly into the duplex. Two boys stand next to each other in the middle of the living room. Two ragged and dirty backpacks rest at their feet. One boy is taller than the other. Their eyes are scared-rabbit wide. They're skinny, all elbows and cheekbones. Their T-shirts are clean, but baggy. As if they reached into Goodwill bags and pulled out the first things their fingers touched.

Tía stands behind them. Pats the taller one's head. "This is Carlos." She does the same pat-head thing to the smaller one. "And Arturo." She says something to them in Spanish. I hear *Diego,* so I assume she just introduced me. They nod. Arturo smiles. Carlos stares.

"Yeah, hi," I say. "So I'm going to my room." Except it's not my room anymore, is it? It's *our* room. I don't correct myself. I'm sure they don't understand anyway.

"Diego," Tía says. "They just arrived. I'm going to make them sandwiches. I'd like you to join us."

"But I'm going to Eric's."

"Do you want me to tell your father you were rude to your cousins?"

I sigh. "Let me set my stuff down."

She hustles the boys into the kitchen, cooing to them in Spanish.

I go to the bedroom. Set my backpack on my bed. Make sure my toy box is where it's supposed to be. Memorize everything else in my room. The pencils on my desk. My drawings on the walls. The stuff on my dresser. If they move something, touch anything, I'll know it. Then there will be hell to pay.

I text Eric, "Cousins here. Not sure when I can come over."

I step into the kitchen. They're eating tuna sandwiches. I don't think I've ever seen anyone eat with that much focus. Like these are the last two tuna sandwiches in existence. I sit next to Tía.

"Immigration processed them sooner than expected," she explains. "Carlos said the shelter in Arizona was over-crowded. They needed to make room for new arrivals. So the kids with American relatives were quickly sent on their way. They were on a bus for eighteen hours. They weren't given much food for the trip. And they had no money to buy any."

That explains the starvation eating.

Carlos, the older one, looks up from his sandwich. He's

got these really intense, predator eyes. I have a feeling he understood some of what our aunt said. He focuses back on his food.

Arturo glances at me every once in a while. He smiles every time. I catch myself smiling back. Can't help it. He looks exactly like my fifth-grade school photo. It's hard to believe this kid who looks like me was living in another country, and I didn't even know he existed.

"How come you and Dad never talk about your family?" I ask. Carlos and Arturo have inhaled their food and are now gulping juice.

Tía fidgets. "It's too sad to remember. To leave your family and home. Then your father wanted you to be American only, Diego. Embrace the country where you were born. Leave the past behind. Start fresh. Maybe that was a mistake. Maybe a wrong decision."

Maybe. I don't know. Sure feels weird at the moment.

Tía gives the boys a tour of the house. It doesn't take long. Just the living room. Bathroom. My bedroom. They stare at the bunk bed. Carlos immediately throws his backpack on the top mattress. Arturo barks what I think is a complaint. But his older brother cuts him off.

Wow. Bully much? Carlos says something else to Arturo. Tía says something to Carlos. He shakes his head.

"What was that all about?" I ask her.

"He's afraid Arturo will fall from the top bunk. I

assured him that won't happen with those wooden bars. But he won't allow it. He's very protective of his younger brother." She heads out. "I'm going to visit the schools. See when they can start." She pats my arm. "I know you'll get along like brothers, Diego."

I take a deep breath. Right.

CHAPTER 10

It's super awkward in my room without Tía. She's our go-between. Our translator. Now we're three strangers staring at each other with nothing to say. Arturo sits on the bottom bunk. Carlos sits next to him.

I have their attention. Might as well try to set some ground rules.

"This is my side of the room," I say, holding my hands out and indicating my bed, desk, and half the closet. "Mine." I point to my chest. "This is your side." I point to the right. "This is my side." I point to the left. I make an *X* with my index fingers. Hope that's a universal Keep Out sign.

They're still staring at me. Are they understanding any of this?

"Get it?" I ask.

Carlos narrows his eyes. Nods.

"You do?" I ask.

"Little," he says. It comes out *leetle*.

"And me," Arturo says.

"Okay. Did you learn English in school?" I ask slowly.

Carlos nods. Arturo looks confused. I'm not sure he understood that.

"So is there anything you want to ask me? Do you have any questions?"

Carlos points at a drawing over my bed. It's my own take on the *Avengers*. The Hulk, Thor, and Captain America are facing off. Iron Man is swooping down with one fist extended. Like he's about to annihilate all of them. "You do that?" he asks.

"Yeah. I'm an artist."

"Cartoon," Arturo says.

"Right. It's a cartoon," I say.

"I like cartoon," he says.

"Oh yeah?" I reach under my bed. Pull out a cardboard box. Kick it to the center of the room. "Here," I say. "Knock yourselves out."

Arturo slowly gets off the bed. Opens the box. Gasps. He says something to Carlos in Spanish. In an instant, Carlos is kneeling on the floor with his younger brother, pawing through my collection of comic books.

"Hey, be careful," I say.

I don't think they hear me. They're too busy turning pages and gawking. Huh. Who knew comic books were a universal language?

With the cousins busy, I slip out and walk to Eric's. He

lives on the outskirts of town. In Seton's only subdivision. As the story goes, some rich dude bought the old lumber mill in town that hadn't been used for like fifty years. He was going to turn it into a posh private school or antique mall or something. In anticipation, a hip coffee shop moved in. A developer built the subdivision. Seton was like this really hot spot for a very short time. Then the rich guy's plans fell through.

So we're still a tiny dot on the dairyland map, with a bar, real estate office, convenience store, cheese factory, hay and feed store, and one very hip coffee shop. Eric's dad works at the community college. It's a long commute. I guess he likes the peace and quiet here. Same reason Dad likes it. That, and he's always had this dream of buying his own dairy someday. He likes cows.

I like Eric's house. It's modern. Shiny appliances in the kitchen. New furniture. Totally unlike our crappy 1960s duplex. But I don't stay long. Just enough to smoke and play a couple of video games. Then I go. I don't want to leave Carlos and Arturo alone in my room for very long. I don't trust them yet. I mean, do we really know why they left Guatemala? Could it be they were actually *in* a drug gang? And they're on the run from Guatemalan narcs? And they've come here undercover to sell drugs? Who's to say, right?

I tiptoe into my room, ready to catch them in my weed. But they're both curled on their beds. The box of comic books is neatly closed. I notice a Spider-Man comic peaking out from under Arturo's pillow.

"Diego." I twist around.

Tía is motioning to me from the hallway.

"They can start school on Monday," she whispers. "Can you walk with them?"

Walking Arturo to the middle school will take extra time. But I'm on her jerk radar, so what can I say? "Okay."

Neither of them wakes up the rest of the night. It takes me forever to get to sleep. I keep listening to them breathe.

ം

Mr. Dawson stops me after English on Friday. "How's the set coming, Diego?"

"Um, I've been thinking it over. And I'm probably not going to do it."

"Really? A week ago you seemed so excited. What happened?"

I shrug. "Complications."

"Anything I can help with?"

And here I thought he didn't care. Potted plants from home and all that. "Not really. Anyway, I thought you wanted to keep it simple."

"I did. But I've invited some colleagues from the drama department at the university. A nice set would make it look more professional. And I loved your drawing."

"Oh yeah?"

"Yeah. It was great. Well, if you can't do it, you can't. I'll check with Ms. Evans. See if she can recommend one or two of her other students. Hey, would you mind if we use your sketch?"

Mind? I totally mind. It's my idea. "I don't know," I say, my thoughts spinning. "It could be that maybe I can do it. There was just this thing I needed to work out."

"Well, let me know soon, okay? There are only five weeks before the performance."

"Sure. Monday. I'll let you know Monday."

I leave English, wondering what it is I need to work out. To get my mind straight, I guess. Find some courage.

I sit with Eric at lunch. Remember what's important— impressing my dad. Going to art school. This has been a really messed-up week. But I can't let it ruin my life.

I go to the office before the bell rings.

"Is Principal Wright in?" I ask the secretary. "It's about the school play."

"Mister Dawson is in charge of the school play," she says primly. "You need to talk to him."

I force myself not to turn around and leave. I tap the counter. "I need to clear something with the principal."

"Okay. Let me check." She disappears deep into the office. Comes back with Mrs. Wright in tow.

"Something wrong, Diego?" Mrs. Wright asks suspiciously.

"No. I, um …" I scratch my forehead. Finally ask her my question.

"Well," she says when I'm finished. "I'm pretty sure the backstage is available to build the sets. But there are issues with safety and liability. I can't let you use power tools, for example. And everything you do will need to be under a teacher's supervision."

"Ms. Evans said she'll do that."

The principal eyes me a long moment. "All right. Tell her to contact me."

"Okay. Thanks."

I scoot out of the office.

Roadblocks. They are wearing me down.

CHAPTER 11

I talk to Ms. Evans in sixth period.

"If you can't use the auditorium," she says, "why don't you make the sets at home? That way you can use the tools you need. I'm still busy with soccer after school for a couple of weeks."

Gee, home is a great idea. Except we have a tiny one-car garage. And now I'll have to okay it with my aunt. She'll have to park on the street. She hates parking on the street.

"Thanks," I say. "I'll think about it."

I want to quit again. But the thought of someone else doing this project really burns me. Makes me feel like a supreme idiot.

I walk home. Tía's in the kitchen reading the newspaper. I wonder why she's not at work, then I remember she took the day off to be with Carlos and Arturo. The TV in the living room is on. I assume that's where they are. I tell her I need the garage and explain why.

"For how long?" she asks. Her lips are pursed.

"Four weeks. Five tops."

"And you'll get extra credit?"

I nod.

"Okay. You can use the garage." She folds the newspaper. "What shall we do with your cousins this weekend? They seem bored already."

"I don't know. Why don't you drive them around?"

"I already did. I was hoping you might spend some time with them."

"I can't. I need to get started on this project."

"Can you get them to help?" she asks.

"They don't know anything about making sets for a play," I say.

"Does it matter? Figure out a way to involve them."

I cross to the refrigerator. "My cousins are not my problem."

"Diego." I can't miss the I'll-tell-your-dad tone in her voice.

I pull a soda out of the fridge and slam the door. "Fine. I'll spend time with them. They're the brothers I never had."

"Are you going to a party tonight?" she asks.

"No." There's one I could go to. But it's at a friend of Tanya's, and I'm sure she'll be there. Seeing her at school is bad enough. I'm not ready to face her at a party. Especially if she brings her elderly boyfriend.

I head for my room. Pass Carlos and Arturo in the living room. Carlos is flipping channels with the remote. They look up at the same time.

"*Hola*," I say.

"Hi," Arturo says with his customary grin.

Carlos gives me his usual stare.

I think about stopping and chatting. But the thought of trying to communicate makes me tired. I go to my room and lie on my bed. Want to get high. Realize I will never be able to smoke again in my room. This had occurred to me before, but now it's a reality. So depressing. Friggin' helpless cousins.

I hear a noise. Arturo is standing in the doorway. He says in halting English, "How … was … school?"

"Terrific," I answer flatly. "*Bueno*."

He nods. Slowly steps inside. Like he's not sure he should be here. Part of me is happy he respects my space. But where else is he supposed to go? "It's okay. This is your room too."

"Comics?" He points under my bed.

"Sure." I pull the box out for him. Open it.

He goes through them. More slowly than before. Pulls out all the Spider-Man. Carries them to his bed.

"You like Spider-Man?" I ask.

He nods fast.

"Yeah. Me too."

"Which you like most?" he asks.

"Iron Man," I answer. He looks at me blankly. I find a comic with Iron Man on the cover. Hold it out. "Iron Man."

"Iron Man," Arturo repeats. "Good."

"Right. Iron Man. Good." Jeez, now I'm starting to talk like him. I need to get high. I text Eric. Ask if I can come over later.

He texts back, "Nope. Mom's birthday."

Crap. Arturo is focused on comics. Carlos is watching TV. I grab the stuff I need from my backpack. Shove it into my hoodie pocket. Slip out of the house. Scoot behind the bushes at the church. Light my pipe. Hang out until I figure Tía is probably wondering where I am. Feel a hundred percent better. Step out of the bushes.

Carlos is standing on the lawn between the sidewalk and the bushes. Staring at me.

"Did you follow me?" I ask. Of course he did. How else did he track me here? "That's not cool, man."

He nods.

Is he agreeing? Does he know what I was doing and approves? Disapproves?

Paranoia runs rampant. He's going to tell Tía. Who will tell Dad. Who will end my life. "Stop staring and say something."

He steps into the enclosure of bushes. Huh? He looks

out at me. Raises two fingers to his lips. As if he's smoking a joint.

Oh. Crap. He knows I'm smoking and he wants some. I don't know what to do. Tía is expecting me to look out for him. He's fourteen. I was smoking when I was fourteen, but still. This doesn't seem quite right.

On the other hand, if I don't give him what he wants, he might tell on me. I don't know anything about this kid. His lifestyle or his friends. Maybe that's how he survived in Guatemala—blackmail and extortion.

What the hell.

I join him. Light my pipe. He smokes without a word. We walk home. Also without a word.

I keep my promise to Tía and entertain the cousins on Saturday. We kick my soccer ball around. I take them on a walking tour of town. Buy them sodas and candy bars at the convenience store. Watch TV. Arturo practices his English on me. He takes in everything like a sponge. Carlos takes in everything too. Only more like a hawk. It creeps me out. At least he doesn't ask for more weed.

By Sunday I'm done babysitting. I deserve a break. I refuse to go to church with Tía and the boys. Plan on spending the morning smoking and thinking about Tanya. But I start thinking about the set.

I force myself to get up. Sit at my desk. Find directions online about how to build them. It doesn't look too complicated. Two-by-four boxes with thin sheets of plywood attached to the fronts. A backdrop made from canvas drop cloths.

I make a list of materials and supplies I'll need. This is going to require a truck. A trip back to Ukiah to a big-box hardware store.

I find the entire play on YouTube. I'm halfway through. Feel a presence behind me. Carlos is sitting on Arturo's bed. Watching. Smiling. Not a big smile, just a slight turn of his lips. I scoot a little out of the way so he has a better view. We laugh at the same spots. It's kind of funny, even though neither of us know what the frig they're talking about.

CHAPTER 12

Oh my God. The bathroom Monday morning. There's only one. Tía and I had a weekday routine. She got up first. Did her thing. Then I had the bathroom to myself. Fine. Now I really have to go. And I have to shower. And it's getting late. And Arturo has been in there *forever*. I pound on the door. "Hey! Hurry up!"

"Okay," comes his soft reply.

I go back to my—*our*—room. Arturo finally wanders in.

"About time," I mutter.

He shrugs.

I run into the bathroom. Oh, gah, it stinks! I open the window.

It's really late by the time I get to the kitchen. Arturo and Carlos are calmly eating cold cereal. Scrubbed and shiny in their new khaki pants and button-down shirts. Tía took them shopping yesterday. Meanwhile, I feel like a nervous wreck. I would love a hit or two. But no stopping at the church this morning with the boys in tow.

"Come on," I tell them. "We need to go."

"You need to eat," Tía says.

"There's no time! We have to stop at the middle school first."

Tía is quiet for a second. "I'll drop Arturo off this morning."

"You will? Awesome." I pour myself a bowl of cereal. Gulp it down. "Come on, Carlos. Chop-chop."

I grab all my stuff from the bedroom. Notice Carlos's backpack on the floor. I pick it up. Toss it to him in the kitchen. "Here," I say. "You'll need this."

He casts a lingering look at his brother. Who jumps up and hugs him. Carlos pets Arturo's head. They hug like they're never going to see each other again.

Yeah, yeah. Come on.

We're finally out the door. Get near the church. Arturo isn't with us, so I think about it. Like for a second. I tug Carlos's sleeve. We slip behind the bushes. I light up. Offer the pipe to him. He shakes his head.

I wonder about his drug-use habits. Maybe he's not a hardcore user. Maybe on Friday he just needed to get his mind off things. After a couple of hits, my thoughts flatten. I forget about the crowded bathroom. About being late for school.

Carlos ventures out of the bushes. I guess he wants to get going. Maybe we should.

The bell rings as we climb the stairs. I take Carlos to the office. The secretary says Mrs. Wright is off doing important principal things. So we stand there. Carlos looks around. Takes in the office and hallway with his hawk vision. His backpack is looped over one shoulder. He keeps tapping the strap.

"It's cool," I tell him. "Everything's cool."

He doesn't smile. Just stares.

Mrs. Wright trots in. "You should have gotten to school much earlier," she scolds me.

"Sorry. Weird morning."

She nods. Then her eyes soften. She must realize this is not a normal situation. "And this is your cousin Carlos?"

"Yeah."

She reaches out her hand. "*Hola*, Carlos." They shake. She starts talking to him in Spanish. Hands him a class schedule. She speaks more Spanish. He nods and says a few words. Then she turns to me. "I want you to be your cousin's escort for the day. Take him to his classes before you go to your own. Here's a permission slip so your teachers won't mark you tardy. All right?"

I take the slip from her. "Okay."

"You'd better get going." She smiles. "*Adios*, Carlos. *Bienvenido*."

We leave the office. I take the schedule from him. His first class is freshman math. "This way," I mutter.

That's how it goes the rest of the morning. I pick him up from class. Take him to his next class. Then it's lunchtime. I can't just leave him to himself. Well, I could, but even I'm not that rude. So I take him to the lunchroom. We get in line together. "Do you have money?" I ask. "*Dinero?*"

He nods. Tía must have given him some bills. There's meat surprise and pizza today. "Get the pizza," I advise. I point at the meat surprise. Slice my finger across my throat and make a gagging sound.

He nods. Points at the pizza when it's his turn.

We buy our food. Sit with Eric, who always brings his lunch.

"Hey, man," I say.

"Hey," Eric says. "This your cousin?"

"Yeah. Carlos, Eric. Eric, Carlos." I take a bite of pizza. Say to Eric, "I'm not sure how much he understands."

"Enough," Carlos says.

I stare at him. "Okay."

He stares back at me. "Okay."

I shake my head. What is with this kid?

I talk to Eric about the supplies I need for the set. He tells me he can probably borrow his dad's pickup. Drive it to Home Depot.

"But not until Saturday," he says.

"Really? That's five more days."

"Sorry. It's a long drive. And I have to work every day this week."

"Fine. Whatever." Yet another setback. But that will still give me about four weeks. Should be enough time. The stuff I saw online seemed pretty basic.

"Hi, Diego."

I twist around. Tanya is standing behind me. Anise is with her. My heart thumps. This is the first time she's spoken to me since we broke up. She looks awesome in her short black skirt and tight T-shirt. "Hi."

"Is this your cousin?" she asks.

"Y-yeah," I stammer. "Carlos."

"I just wanted to say hello." She wags her fingers at him. "Hello, Carlos."

"Hi," Carlos says. I'm not surprised when he stares at her, since he stares at everything. But I am surprised by the slight lecherousness.

CHAPTER 13

Hey," I scold Carlos. "That's my girlfriend. Don't look at her like that."

"*Was* your girlfriend," Tanya corrects me. "Your cousin is cute."

"Definitely cute." Anise giggles.

Are they serious? Teasing? Either option pisses me off. "Leave him alone. He's only fourteen."

"Fifteen," Carlos says.

"What?" I say.

"Really?" Tanya says. "You're just a freshman? You look a lot older. Welcome to Seton." She sits next to him. "So you came here from Guatemala?"

"Yes," Carlos says.

"Why? What happened?"

He proceeds to tell her—in broken but understandable English—how a drug gang threatened to kill him and his brother if they didn't join up. How the two of them took a bus. Then crossed a river. Walked for days. Then hopped a train in Mexico called *La Bestia*—the Beast. His eyes kind of glaze over at the mention of the train.

"Then what happened?" Tanya prods.

He shakes his head. "People fall off. Get killed under wheels. Some people robbed."

"That's awful," Anise says.

"After train we walk. My father pay coyote. Coyote get us to border. In back of van. No windows. No air. Drop us so immigration find us. Then here I am." His face is pale. His hand shakes as he picks up his pizza. He sets it down again without eating.

We're all quiet a moment. Absorbing his story.

Finally, Tanya says, "That's amazing. You're so lucky to have family here to take you in."

Carlos slowly nods. Stares at his plate.

Why didn't I ask him all this when he first got here? I feel like such an asshole. It could be that he's lying. But I don't think so. I could tell he was reliving it as he spoke. No wonder he seems paranoid all the time. Watches everything like a hawk. He's probably looking for the next crappy thing to happen.

"Well, we'd better go," Tanya says to Anise. "Nice meeting you, Carlos."

"Bye," Carlos says. He ogles her again as she walks away.

I don't blame him. She looks good from this angle. But

I'm not feeling *that* sorry for him. "Didn't you hear me, Carlos? I said don't look at her like that."

"Why not?" Eric says. "Like Tanya said, you guys aren't together anymore."

That's right, we're not. And that is totally wrong. I slap the table and jump up. "I'll be right back." I chase after Tanya. Catch up to her in the hallway. "Hey," I say.

She stops. Crosses her arms. "What do you want?"

Anise gives me a withering look before she heads to the restroom.

"I want to … thank you for being nice to my cousin," I say. "That was … nice."

"Sure. Whatever."

"So how are you?" I fight the urge to wrap her in my arms. Hold her against me.

"Fine."

"Are you still going out with that guy?"

"Diego. That's really none of your business. You and I broke up."

"No, you broke up with me. Big difference. I still like you. I want us to be together."

"Don't do this, please?" She walks away.

"Do what, Tanya? Tell you that I care about you?" I yell.

She disappears inside the restroom.

Kids stare as they maneuver around me in the hallway. "What?" I bark at them.

I slump back to the cafeteria. Plop into my chair. Lean back and cross my arms.

"Hey," Eric says. "Did you know Carlos wants to be an engineer? He studied English because he wants to go to college in the U.S."

"Well, good for him. He'll be the son my dad always wanted."

Carlos glances at me. Then back at his tray.

"Sorry. I'm having a bad day. Feel free to stare at Tanya if you want. Ask her out. Have sex with her. I don't care." I glance at the clock. The bell is about to ring. "Come on. I need to get you to your next class."

Last period, I show Ms. Evans my supply list. She glances at it. Says, "Good. Thanks." Nothing else.

Carlos and I leave to pick up Arturo. The middle school and high school let out at the same time. They're just two blocks from each other. Arturo runs into his brother's arms. They hug like they haven't seen each other in an eon. Come on, guys, get a grip. Then it occurs to me. Today is probably the longest they've been separated since they left home. I take a deep breath. Want to get high.

ॐ

The rest of the week plods by. I'm smoking less. Irritated more. I yell at everyone to get out of the bathroom. Then feel guilty for yelling. It's not their fault we have one friggin' toilet. Carlos and I drop off Arturo in the mornings.

71

We talk a little. Just chit-chat. It's like neither of us knows what to say. I envy how Tanya got him to open up so easily. Maybe it's a girl thing.

Carlos gets himself to his classes. But we still hang out at lunch. I hope he makes his own friends soon. I know that's a lot to expect. He and Eric get along. They both like math and computers. I talk to Tía about getting him a laptop. I don't want him borrowing mine.

Saturday rolls around. I am stoked about getting away for a while. Just me and Eric. His dad's pickup. A trip to Home Depot. And a big fat joint. I'm in a good mood.

Then Tía says, "Why don't you take Carlos with you?"

My good mood goes *pfffft*.

He's sitting right next to me at the kitchen table. I can't exactly say no way in hell. "Uh … I'm not sure there's room in Eric's truck."

"Make room. Squeeze together. Carlos hasn't seen Ukiah yet. Or Home Depot."

She speaks to Carlos in Spanish. He shrugs. Nods.

"What about Arturo?" I ask.

"I'll watch him," she says.

Wow. Fun.

CHAPTER 14

Eric picks us up. I make Carlos sit in the middle. He gapes at the redwood forests on either side of the highway. Eric asks me about the stuff I need to get. I pull out my sketchpad with my list. I've drawn a few plans on the page next to it.

Carlos glances at the drawings. Nods. Like he just figured something out. "Shakespeare," he says.

"Yeah. How did you know?"

"We watched. On computer."

"Oh yeah. *A Midsummer Night's Dream.* I'm making the sets."

"Sets," he repeats. He points at one of my drawings. "How big?"

"Like a redwood tree." I point outside the truck.

Carlos laughs. "Too tall."

"Well, duh. It will just be the start of the trunk. The bottom of the tree. Get it? Two on each side of the stage.

Then I'll paint more trees on the backdrop." I point at another sketch.

"How hang it?" Carlos asks.

"The backdrop? I don't know. I'm hoping there's something on the stage I can use."

"You not check first?"

"No." I close my sketchbook. Don't care if Carlos is along. I need to get high. I pull out a joint. Light it. Take a long drag. Reach across Carlos and hand it to Eric.

"Thanks, man," Eric says. He inhales. Hands it to Carlos. Carlos shakes his head. His shoulders are straight. He stares ahead with wide eyes.

I take the joint. "What's wrong? I've seen you smoke."

Silence.

"Maybe he's worried about getting arrested," Eric says. "He probably has to be careful about stuff like that. Or he might get deported."

"Is that right?" I ask Carlos.

His jaw is tight. He's either about to explode or cry. He nods stiffly.

I slam my head against the backrest. Inhale one more time. Stub out the joint. Throw it out the window. "There. Feel better?"

"Thank you," he says.

I sigh. "Whatever."

"Sorry I come with you."

"It's okay. Just chill. You're fine. We're fine. Right, Eric?"

"Totally fine," Eric says.

ॐ

We get to Home Depot. I find the sheets of plywood I need. Two-by-fours. Screws and nails. A couple of canvas drop cloths. Paint. Brushes. The bill is over two hundred dollars. I'm glad I brought weed money. The fifty bucks Mr. Dawson promised won't go far.

I treat Carlos and Eric to In-N-Out burgers. That cheers Carlos up quite a bit. He actually smiles.

"Good, huh?" I say.

"Yes. Good."

"So you want to be an engineer?" I ask. "And do what with it?"

He sets down his burger. Fiddles his fingers together. "Make. Things."

"Mechanical engineer?" Eric says.

"Yes," Carlos says. "Mechanical engineer."

"Have you ever made things, like with wood? Have you used tools?" I ask.

He shrugs. "I help fix house in Guatemala. Make repair."

"Awesome. How would you like to help us build the sets?"

He takes a moment to think about it. "Okay."

ॐ

I feel pretty good on the drive home. Even without a smoke

booster. There will be three of us working on the sets. Which I figure ups the chances of them getting done. I'll need to sell more weed to make up the money I spent. I'll ride to Convoy's tomorrow. Get more product.

We unload the stuff in the garage, and Eric heads home.

Tía is in the living room watching a movie. Arturo comes running down the hallway when he hears us. The brothers share a long reunion hug. A kid I've never seen before wanders out behind Arturo.

"Who are you?" I ask.

"Brandon," he says.

"Arturo made a friend at school," Tía says. She grabs her purse. "Now that you're home, I need to go shopping. Watch the boys, okay?"

"Sure. Fine."

She leaves, and I get this queasy feeling in my stomach. "What have you and Brandon been doing?" I ask Arturo.

"Playing."

"In the bedroom?"

"Yes," he says.

I stride into my room. My heart stops.

The toy box is in the middle of the floor. The lid is open. The stuffed tiger, Xbox, and other toys are sitting next to it. My stash of weed and scale are right there. In clear view.

"You sell weed," Brandon says behind me.

I want to strangle him. But I take my anger out on Arturo. "I said to stay out of my stuff! That side of the closet is mine!"

"Do not yell at him," Carlos says. Then he's staring at the bag. The scale. His jaw drops. "You *sell* drugs?"

"Um, yeah," I say. "But it's not a big deal."

His face turns red. He curls his fingers into fists. "This is what we get away from."

"I know! But this is different." I step back as he raises his fist to slug me. "Calm down, man! It's just a side thing. Like a part-time job."

"Carlos!" Arturo yells, tugging his brother's arm. "*Lo siento!*" He talks fast in Spanish. Carlos lowers his arm. But his face is still screwed up in anger. He grabs the bag of weed. Carries it down the hallway.

"Hey!" I follow him. "What are you doing?"

He marches into the bathroom. I try to grab it from him. "That's mine! You have no right—"

He swings the bag away from me, out of reach. He shoves me against the tub. I tumble through the shower curtain and into the tub. The curtain tears off its hooks and falls around me. I watch in horror as Carlos upends the bag. And dumps my precious weed into the toilet. The finest weed the Emerald Triangle has to offer.

"You idiot!" I scream as he flushes the toilet. "I'll kill you!"

I scramble out of the tub. Grab the front of his T-shirt. Push him against the doorframe.

He doesn't try to get away. "*You* the idiot," he spits in my face. "I kill *you*." His hawk eyes are filled with calm resolve. He will. He'll kill me.

I let him go. Hold up my hands. "Okay. Forget it."

I bump his shoulder as I march past him. Back to my room. I return everything to the box. Shove it in the closet.

Arturo is in the hallway, sobbing.

"Who do you buy your weed from?" Brandon asks, standing next to me. "It looks like good stuff."

"How would you know good weed? And it's none of your business who I buy it from." I notice the corner of a plastic baggie peaking out of his pants pocket. Remember there should be one left in the toy box. I yank the bag out of his pocket. "You little creep. Go home. Don't come back here again."

"That was mine!"

"Go home! Now!"

He scurries away. "Bye, Arturo," he says, "See you at school."

I don't think Arturo heard him. His head is buried in his brother's chest. They're both sitting on the floor, crying.

CHAPTER 15

Cousin fail. Drug fail. Tía isn't back from shopping yet. But I can't stay here. Not with Carlos wanting to kill me. And Arturo's sobs making me want to repeatedly stab myself with a pencil. I wonder if Carlos will tell our aunt. I don't think so. Growing up around drug gangs, he probably knows not to rat.

I jump on my bike. Pedal fast. It's foggy. The moisture feels like a wet slap on my face. I repeat *I am an asshole, I am an asshole* with every pump of my legs.

But am I an asshole? Really? I didn't invite them to live with us. Yes, their lives have been crappy. They went through all kinds of pain to get here. But that's not my fault. Plus, it's not like I left my stuff out in the open. I didn't smoke in the house when they were around. I clearly told Arturo that was my side of my closet. Off-limits.

That snotty Brandon kid. He probably saw the toy box. Told Arturo to open it.

I reach the hill that leads to Convoy's. Turn up Convoy's

road. Hadn't planned on it. I really just wanted to get out of the house. Go for a ride. But I need the weed—for myself, for the income. I'll find another place to stash it. Maybe the garage. I stop the bike for a second. Send him a text. Start pedaling again.

The forest is even darker in the fog. No light streaming through the canopy. It's hushed. Creepy. I only hear my breathing. The *click-click-click* of the bike's wheels. The squish of tires through mud. If a T-Rex suddenly appeared from behind the trees, it wouldn't surprise me.

Convoy's house and the junk scattered around it look equally bland in the dimness. Tires, an old sink, a rusting VW bug. The pit bull and Rottweiler scream out from the side of the house. I stand perfectly still. Wait till they've finished barking and growling and sniffing. They decide they remember me and trot off.

I give the secret knock. Do it a couple more times. Convoy finally comes to the door. He's wearing an industrial-looking apron. Rubber gloves.

"Hey," he says. "You should have let me know you were coming."

"I sent a text."

"Oh. I had the music up pretty loud." He opens the door wider. "I was just whipping up a new batch of ice." He takes off the gloves. Closes the door behind me. "Sales must be good if you're out of weed already."

I shrug. Don't feel like explaining.

"The usual?" he asks.

"Yeah. But I don't have money with me. I was just in the neighborhood."

"Right." He shakes his head. "Not only do I not do credit, my prices have gone up. The cost of fertilizer went through the roof."

"I was hoping just this once. You know me. I'm good for it."

He laughs. "Dude, if we're not related, then I don't know you. Not really."

"Well, would you sell me a few ounces?" I ask.

"I'm a wholesaler."

"A joint?" I practically beg.

"Get out of here."

I head to the door. Then he says, "Diego, wait a second. How much cash do you have on you?"

I pull everything out of my pockets. "Four hundred."

"I want you selling my crystal. Do that, and I'll front you half a pound of weed for your four hundred."

I close my eyes. I don't want to sell meth. But I can't afford my own weed without the money I make from selling. Let alone art school. I take a deep breath. "Okay. Fine." I hand him the cash.

Convoy gives me a Santa Claus's grungy-brother grin. "Cool." He disappears inside the house. Returns with a paper sack. Tells me what to charge for the meth. Then he sends me on my way. "You owe me, little brother. Full payment in two weeks. Or I send my unfriendly minions after you." He slams the door.

༄

I didn't bring my backpack. So I grip the bag of drugs while I ride. I pray a sheriff doesn't pull me over. Search me. Weed is one thing. Meth is a whole new level of illegal. I hate this. Hate that I have it. I think I'll hide it. Or throw it away. Pay Convoy from what I make selling the weed. Even if I only break even this time. That's fine.

I ride my bike into the garage. I'm so nervous my hands are shaking. I glance around. Dad built high shelves along three walls. They're loaded with boxes. I grab a ladder. Find a box in a corner. It's dusty. Cobwebby. Full of holiday decorations we don't use anymore. I shove the bag inside.

I walk into the kitchen. Tía is putting groceries away. She glares at me. "Why did you leave the boys alone?"

"I wanted to go for a ride. Anyway, Carlos is fifteen, not fourteen. He doesn't need a sitter."

"But they're still new here. This is still strange to them." She frowns at me.

At least it doesn't sound like Carlos told her what happened.

"Your father called," Tía says. "He's coming home tonight."

"Oh yeah?" I'm glad he's coming home. I want to see him. But maybe Carlos will blab. Crap. I need to smoke. I have a little weed in my backpack. Which is in my room. I don't want to face Carlos right now. But I'll have to eventually.

I hike up my big-boy pants. Go back there. Arturo is sitting on the floor. Playing with Legos. Carlos is sitting at his desk. Reading a textbook. Writing in his new binder.

Arturo cowers like a guilty puppy when he sees me. "Sorry," he says.

"That's okay, little dude." I pat his head. "You can play with my Legos."

"He mean from before," Carlos says. "He sorry about what happen."

"Yeah, I don't think that was entirely his fault. You should probably tell him not to hang out with Brandon anymore. The kid is a budding sociopath."

"I already tell him," Carlos says. I feel his eyes on me as I grab my backpack. "Where do you go?" he asks.

"Out."

He's got this pining look on his face that I totally recognize. Unbelievable.

"The church," I say. "Want to come with?"

He says something to Arturo. We're out the door.

CHAPTER 16

I hand the pipe to Carlos. "So smoking helps you de-stress," I say.

He nods.

"But you don't like when people sell it. You realize that doesn't make sense," I tell him.

He shrugs. Looks a little sheepish. "I know. Today … seeing all that drug. It made me afraid. I must not get arrested. Must not go back."

"Yeah. I get it. I won't keep it in the house anymore."

"It remind me of my sister. She do too many drugs."

"Sister? You mean I have another cousin?" I ask.

He looks away. "She go with gang. She overdose. Died."

"Oh, crap. I'm sorry, man." Carlos stares into the distance. I want to change the subject. "So what do you think of Seton so far?"

"Too many cows."

I laugh.

"School good. Food good. And I not so …" He hunches his shoulders up around his ears.

"Nervous?"

"*Sí.* So nervous." He looks around. "No one ever catch you here?"

"Not yet."

"We should go?" he asks.

"Yeah. We should go."

Dad's pickup is in the driveway when we get home. He's holding Arturo. He sets him down when he sees us. He gives me a quick hug, then he hugs Carlos like forever. They speak in Spanish. I watch Carlos. Like he said, he isn't so stiff anymore. He smiles more easily. His eyes don't dart around like a hawk's. And I don't think it's just because of the weed he just smoked.

Tía has made a feast. Everyone talks in English—for my benefit. I tell them it's okay to speak Spanish. They take me up on it. I know there's a lot Dad wants to learn about his family.

Dad wraps his arm around me after dinner. He pulls me into the living room, away from everyone. "How's school?"

"Fine."

"How are things with your cousins?"

I shrug. "Okay."

"You understand they may be with us for a long time?"

I hadn't really thought about it. "I guess."

"And my brother has no money to offer us," he says.

"Okay." What is he getting at?

"Diego." He lowers his arm. "I can no longer save money for your education. There is extra food to buy. Clothing. Other expenses. And I will want to help with their college too. It will have to be community college for all of you. Unless you get scholarships."

I stare at him.

"I must do this," he continues. "They're family. My brother would do the same for you. And there may be some legal fees. To help keep them in the U.S." He pats my arm. "You are a good boy. I know you understand." Then he says, "I saw the wood in the garage. Is that for your little art project?"

My little art project. No art school.

"Will they reimburse you?" Dad asks. "Do you need money?"

I shake my head.

He reaches into his pocket. Presses a twenty-dollar bill into my hand. "I'm very tired. I'm going to bed."

He slumps down the hallway to his bedroom. I stand there. Hear Carlos, Arturo, and Tía laughing in the kitchen. I grab my phone. Trot out the front door. Call Eric. He picks up.

"Are you alone?" I ask.

"Yeah. What's up?"

"I got some new stuff from Convoy. I need to unload it."

He's quiet a second. "Oh man. It's the ice, isn't it? I don't want any. I mean, I'd like to, but—"

"That's okay. Do you know anyone? I'll cut you in."

"Maybe. I'll think about it and text you back."

I hang up. Try to remember any customers who've ever asked for meth. I text everyone I have numbers for. Except Tanya. I'm not interested in contributing to her drug habit. Even if she wanted to hear from me.

A response comes while I'm still outside. Alan from school. He lives down the street. That will be easy. Then I get two quick texts from Seton High School football players. They give me the same address. A party house. Perfect. Maybe I can sell weed there too.

I go back inside. Dad's already in bed. He won't be a problem. Tía and the boys are watching TV. I head to my room. Dump out my backpack and carry it to the garage. Grab all the drugs from the box and shove them into the pack. Put the ladder away. Turn to leave.

Carlos is standing in the kitchen doorway.

I freeze. We stare at each other. "Is this when you kill me?" I ask.

"Garage is part of house. You get arrested. Maybe we get arrested too. You think about that?"

No. I didn't think about that. But my cousins getting deported back to Guatemala is not a terrible idea at the moment. Having my normal life back is not a terrible idea. Dad saving money for my college again is a terrific idea.

Tía joins him in the doorway. "What are you two doing?"

I hesitate. "Talking about the sets. Carlos is going to help me."

"That's nice. Do you want ice cream?" she asks.

"No thanks," I say.

Carlos shakes his head. Tía returns to the kitchen.

"I'm out of here." I throw the backpack over my shoulder. "I have a college fund to support. If Tía asks where I am, tell her Eric had an emergency. I had to help him with something."

He narrows his eyes.

"Please?"

He nods.

CHAPTER 17

I text Alan when I reach the sidewalk. He's waiting for me on his front porch. "Sorry, Diego," he whispers. "I thought I could find the money. But my mom is out. She took her purse with her."

"Great." Then I ask, "Need any weed?"

"Yeah. But I don't have money for that either."

"Fine. Whatever," I say.

I head for the jock party. It's at a notorious party house. I don't know who owns it. The place used to be a working dairy. Now it's overrun with weeds. The windows of the old farmhouse are covered with sheets instead of curtains. The roof sags.

I text Caleb, the football player, when I'm a block away. He doesn't text back. High school kids are milling around outside. I know a lot of them. Music is blasting. I don't see Caleb. Find him inside. On the couch. Making out with Eliza Jacobs.

"Caleb." I kick his foot to get his attention.

He looks up. "It's about time, man."

I tell him what he owes me.

"That much?" He digs around in his pocket. Pulls out some bills. "I've only got half." He looks pleadingly at Eliza. She shakes her head. "Hey, Simmons!" he yells across the room. "Can I borrow—"

"No way," the guy says. "You owe me from last time. Be cool and stick to beer."

"Dang," Caleb mutters. "I'm good for it, Diego. I swear. I'll pay you Monday."

"No credit. Where's Titus? He texted he wants some."

"He left already."

"Are you kidding me?" I roll my eyes. "Jock asswipes."

"What did you say?" Caleb says.

"Asswipes. I said you're jock asswipes." Of course it's a stupid thing to say. These guys are way bigger than me. Trained bullies. But I'm stone sober and extremely pissed off.

Caleb jumps off the couch. Gets in my face. He shoves me. I shove him back.

"Diego!" It's Tanya. She gets between Caleb and me. "Stop it!"

Caleb stares at her. Then he looks at me. He slowly smiles. "Oh yeah. You guys used to be an item. That must suck for you." He laughs. Eliza pulls him back onto the couch.

Tanya tugs me out the back door. "What are you doing here?"

"Why? Is there a reason I shouldn't be here?" I ask.

"Because I asked them ahead of time. I didn't want to run into you," Tanya says.

"Oh."

She studies my eyes. "You're not even high."

"Tell me about it. I'm selling," I say.

"At a jock party? This isn't your usual crowd."

"I'm not selling my usual stuff."

"Why, what are you selling?" Her eyes widen. "Oh my God. You're selling Convoy's crystal."

"I'd better go," I say. "Your boyfriend's probably wondering where you are."

"Wait." She grabs my hand. "We aren't going out anymore."

"You're here alone?" I ask.

Her smile—and her hands sliding up and down my arm—shoots an electrical bolt through my head and out my feet. She leads me back into the house. She asks for meth. I give it to her. She asks if I want to try it. I don't even hesitate. Because tonight I do. I really do.

Damn.

Just ... damn.

I have never felt a rush like this. I feel so awake. Smart. Amazing. And I'm happy to be doing this with Tanya.

Because she is my love. My true love. And we're back together. And that's all I want. I just want Tanya. My Apegirl. Together we'll conquer the evil alien monkeys. Everything will be cool. Everything will perfect.

I'm up all night. It's morning when I finally get home.

I crash.

ॐ

I open my eyes. It's dark. Huh? How? It can't be night again. Can it?

I hear, "He's awake."

The overhead light switches on. It's too bright. I squint. Block the light with my hand. Dad looms over me. Frowning.

"Hey," I say. I feel sick. I need water. "What's going on?"

"Sit up," he says angrily.

Why is he so mad? I try to remember. I was at that party. With Tanya. We did some meth. Maybe a lot of meth. How did I end up there? That's right. I was selling. Or trying to sell.

My backpack!

I sit up. Glance around the room. Don't see it. Push down a rising panic.

"Looking for this?" Dad holds up my pack.

"That's mine." I reach for it. He pulls it away.

"What is wrong with you, Diego?" Dad yells. "You're selling drugs? How can you be so stupid!"

My head's not on straight. I press a shaking hand to my forehead. Wish I could disappear. Wish I could smoke.

He throws the backpack on my bed. I can tell by the way it lands that it's empty. I groan. "Dad, you just got me killed. I owe him money."

"Who do you owe money?" Dad asks. "How much?"

I shake my head. "A few thousand dollars. I can't tell you who."

"You *will* tell me," he growls. "Or I will call the police and have you arrested."

"You wouldn't do that. They might deport Carlos and Arturo. Anyway, I'm sure you already destroyed the evidence."

He pulls my desk chair in front of me. Sits. Grabs my chin. Forces me to look at him. "This is the very thing your cousins risked their lives to get away from. You are so lucky. You have so much. But you're willing to throw it away by selling drugs?" He squeezes my chin. "Why, Diego?"

I knock his hand away. "Money! Why else?"

"What do you need so much money for?"

"For college! Art school!" I hold his eyes. "You don't want me to go. But I do. More than anything. I'll pay for it myself."

"Do you use the drugs you sell?" he asks.

I look away.

He shakes his head. Pushes the chair back. Gets to his feet.

"What are you going to do?" I ask.

"I don't know. For now you stay in your room. You only go to school. Then you come home. I'm canceling my next job."

Hearing him say that hurts more than anything. We don't have enough money for him to not work.

He marches out of my room.

I lie back down. Feel sick. Exhausted. Carlos and Arturo creep in a few minutes later. Climb into their beds. I should be mad at Carlos. I'm sure he had something to do with Dad finding my backpack. But I'm not capable of doing anything more than sleep.

CHAPTER 18

I get up early Monday morning before anyone else. I search my pants, hoodies, jackets. Every pocket. Every drawer. No weed. Also no phone. Dad must have taken that too. Crap. There are a zillion texts to and from buyers on my phone. Texts with Convoy. I never checked if Eric sent me any names.

I use the bathroom. Shower until the water runs cold.

I'm starving. Haven't eaten in over a day. I pour a huge bowl of cereal. Carlos wanders in. Still in his pj's. "I used all the hot water," I tell him. "Might want to wait to shower."

He stands there. Must have something on his mind. I know I do. "Did you give Dad my backpack?" I ask.

He nods. "You drop it on floor. When you come in Sunday."

"You're an asshole."

"I do not know what that means," he says.

"Figure it out."

He lowers his gaze. "Before we leave Guatemala my father say, 'Protect your brother.' So that is what I do. That is what I must do. Do you understand?"

"I've never had a brother. But I get the concept. I still think you're an asshole."

"What would you do? If you were me?" he asks.

I think about it. I'd probably do the same thing. Get rid of all threats. But I don't tell him that. Don't want to give him the satisfaction of being right.

I'm like an outcast in the house. Everyone avoids me. Won't even look at me.

Dad is waiting at the door as the three of us leave for school. "Come straight home," he tells me. "Then we'll talk about what to do."

"Fine. I'd like my phone back, please."

"No," he says.

We walk by the church. I'm desperate to get high. I am in pain to get high. At least Tanya and I are back together. I'll pick her up tomorrow. Carlos and Arturo can walk by themselves.

I hang around Tanya's locker. She saunters down the hallway. Smiles. I smile. She kisses me. I kiss her. My heart ping-pongs.

"You are amazing." I hug her. Don't want to let go. "I had such a good time on Saturday."

"Me too." She pulls away. Opens her locker.

"Do you know you're the only thing in my life that doesn't completely suck right now?"

"Why?" She closes her locker. I wrap my arm around her. We walk to first period. I tell her about Carlos giving Dad my backpack. Getting rid of all my drugs.

"When will you get more?" she asks.

"Um, didn't you hear me? I owe Convoy a lot of money. I can't afford more drugs."

Tanya is quiet. "Henry might let you sell on credit. Do you want me to ask him? I can text him right now if you want."

"Henry? Your mom's douchebag of a boyfriend?"

"He's not that bad," she says.

"I don't know. Maybe. I'll think about it."

We sit together in English. More Shakespeare. Ugh. The time drags. I can't remember the last time I sat through first period sober. It sucks.

I would love to have a stash again. I could keep it away from the house. Away from Dad and Carlos. Maybe in my locker at school. Or at Eric's house. He'll let me if I give him freebies.

I think about what Dad will say when I get home. He probably wants me to tell him about Convoy. I can't snitch. Everyone hates a rat. I could end up dead. For sure no one would ever trust me to sell again.

I look at the clock. Still twenty minutes to go. I jiggle

my leg. Tap my desk. Tanya glances at my tapping fingers. I spread them flat on my desk and slide down into my seat.

The bell finally rings. I jump up. Whisper in Tanya's ear, "Do you have any smoke?"

She shakes her head.

"Diego," Mr. Dawson says. "Can I talk to you?"

Tanya waves to me. I watch her walk away.

"What's up?" I ask him.

"You seem a little scattered. Everything okay?"

"Yeah. Everything's great. You?"

He smirks. "I'm fine. How are the sets coming along?"

The sets. The sets! It feels like a month since I was at Home Depot. "Um. I got the materials on Saturday. The wood and stuff."

"Okay. When will they be done? The sooner we can rehearse with everything in place, the better," he says.

"I thought I had until the end. You know, the day of the play."

He shakes his head. "The actors need to become familiar with the stage. The physical obstacles." He sighs. "Diego, are you still up for this? If you aren't, then tell me now."

"I'm up for it!" Though I'm not sure why. "I'll work on it this week. I promise."

"Okay." He pulls out his wallet. "Here." He hands me fifty dollars.

"I don't have the receipt with me."

"Show me tomorrow. I know wood is expensive."

"Thanks," I say.

I walk to second period. The money burns a hole in my pocket. I try to think of anyone I can buy weed from. Can't. Because I'm *that* guy. I'm Seton High School's supplier.

I slip into second period as the bell rings. Sit next to Eric. Whisper, "You got anything?"

"No." He squints. "I thought you got a new stash. I kept texting you Saturday night. You never got back to me."

That's right. He doesn't know. "Long story. I'll tell you later."

Mrs. Albert shushes us.

I tap my fingers. Jiggle my legs. Math lasts longer than English.

ဢ

Tanya and I walk to lunch. We sit alone at a back table. I see Carlos standing in the cafeteria line. He's glancing around. This is the first lunch I haven't waited for him. I was hoping he'd have a friend by now.

Tanya pulls out her phone. "Want me to text him now?"

"Who?"

"Henry." She sighs. "He can probably set you up tonight. You can come over. We can get high."

"I'm grounded," I say.

"Are you kidding me? Then sneak out."

"Don't think I can. Dad has me on a tight leash."

"You are such a wimp, Diego. Why are you so afraid of your father?"

I'm still watching Carlos. Now he's carrying his tray around the cafeteria. He finds an empty seat.

Oh no. Carlos, you idiot. Not the jock's table. You're a fifteen-year-old Guatemalan kid who barely speaks English. They will shred you.

CHAPTER 19

I turn my stricken gaze from Carlos back to Tanya. My cousin is not my problem. If he's going to fit in, he needs to learn the school hierarchy on his own. I can't hold his hand forever.

"So, I'm texting Henry," Tanya says.

A movement catches my eye. Caleb is picking the apple off Carlos's tray.

Come on, Carlos. Use your survival instincts. Get out of there.

He doesn't leave. He reaches for his apple.

I jump up.

"Where are you going?" Tanya asks.

"I'll be right back." I walk as quickly as I can without looking like I care. "Hey," I say to Caleb. "How's it going?"

He's grinning. Tossing the apple in the air. "I hear you and this little wetback are related."

"Yep," I say. "This is my cousin Carlos. He's as wet as they come." I slap Carlos's back. Tug his shirt. "Come on, cousin. Let's let Caleb and the boys eat their lunch."

"No," he spits out. He reaches again for his apple.

Caleb laughs as he pulls it away.

"They're terrible apples," I tell Carlos. "Zero flavor. Like soggy plastic. You don't want it." My hand is still on his back.

I can feel his muscles flinch. Tighten. The same muscles that must have flinched and tightened every scary day of his recent life.

I whisper in his ear. "I know you're angry. You have a right to be. But this is not the person or the time to take revenge. Trust me. Now come on."

He slowly gets up. Grabs his tray. I lead him to the back of the cafeteria. Away from the jocks. Away from Tanya. He eats like a robot, tears dripping down his cheeks onto his tuna casserole.

"I miss my family," he says. "I miss home."

"I know, man," I say. "I know."

✺

I draw in sixth period. A bunch of Apemen battling an army of evil alien monkeys. Art is a high for me. Not as good as weed, but better than nothing.

I see Tanya after sixth period. "It's all set up," she says.

"What's all set up?" I ask.

She rolls her eyes. "Henry. He's bringing stuff for you tonight."

"I told you I can't get away."

"Yes you can."

"Uh, no I can't!" I look her in the eyes. Something has been clicking into place since lunch. "You broke up with me. Like, completely. No hesitation. The second I start selling meth, you want to be my girlfriend again. What's wrong with this picture?"

"Nothing's wrong with it."

"You're a tweaker, Tanya. You want free drugs. I'm really sorry about that. It makes me very sad. But I don't think I can save you anymore."

She throws her hands up. "I don't *want* you to save me! That's why I broke up with you in the first place."

"Yeah, I know. Guess I didn't get it then. But I do now. You have to make your own mistakes."

"So you're breaking up with me?" she says.

I shrug. "Yeah."

ॐ

I walk home with Carlos after school. We pick up Arturo on the way.

Dad and I talk at the kitchen table. Thankfully, he doesn't yell. I don't think I could handle him yelling right now. He figured out who my supplier is from my text messages. We come up with two options. My choice is to pay Convoy what I owe him and be done with it. Dad wants to call in an anonymous tip to the sheriff's office.

"No one will ever know who called," Dad says. "It won't get back to you."

"But he's not a bad guy," I explain. "I hate to see him land in prison because of me. He's just trying to make a living."

"By recruiting boys to sell drugs? And if that's a good way to make a living, maybe I should stop working. Make drugs here in the kitchen. Do you think that's a good idea?"

I sigh. "No."

"I'll decide later," Dad says. "Go do your homework."

"Is it okay if I work on the sets for the play?"

"Yes. Fine."

I get up to leave.

"Diego," he says. "I'm going to try to find work around here. Maybe as a dairy hand. It may pay less. But I think it's important to be home. I just wanted you to know."

"Okay." Personally, I think that's an excellent idea. "Dad, uh, I could use your help with those sets. If you have a minute."

In the garage, I mark two-by-fours with a tape measure. Dad cuts them with the circular saw. He's fearless with that thing. Which is great, because it scares the crap out of me. He teaches Carlos and me how to use it. Carlos and I screw the frame together. We have one box made by the time Tía calls us for dinner.

She's made mac and cheese with cheddar she brought home from the cheese factory. It's awesomely delicious. Arturo tries to tell a joke he learned at school. The joke isn't very funny. But watching him tell it while waving his hands around is hilarious.

I try to do homework. But I'm craving a smoke. It's probably a good thing Dad still has my phone. Because I'd find someone.

I grab my sketchbook. Draw. Think about art school. How I'm going to get there. I will. Somehow I will.

೪

The actors are hamming it up. I've seen them rehearse twice. This is the real deal, with a real audience. My family is out there: Dad, Tía, Carlos, and Arturo. Eric too. I can't see them from here.

I'm standing next to the stage. Or "the wing" as Mr. Dawson calls it. I've learned a lot of stage lingo in the past few days. He asked me to help move the sets and props around during the show. I also think he wants me here in case something breaks and needs a quick fix. That's not going to happen. I may have gotten them done a week later than he wanted. But between Carlos helping, and Dad supervising, they're pretty sturdy.

Steph Miller scoots up next to me. She's decked out in a costume. Playing one of the characters. "Are you going to the after-party?" she whispers.

"Nope."

"I doubt Tanya will be there. It's at Mister Dawson's house."

"I know. Still not going," I say.

She shrugs. Rushes on stage.

The reason I'm not going is because I'm still grounded for life for selling drugs. A huge bummer. But at least Convoy's henchmen never got to me. Dad decided to make that anonymous phone call to the sheriff's office. Except before he got around to it, Convoy's meth lab blew up. He got busted. Maybe it's karma. I don't know. I still feel a little sorry for him. I definitely miss his weed.

The wedding scene finally comes up. Puck gives his speech. Then the play is over. The audience claps and cheers. Actors bow. More clapping. Mr. Dawson thanks different people. Then he says, "And a special thank you to Seton junior Diego Silva for the incredible sets." He waves me over.

Are you freaking kidding me? I shake my head.

Come on, he mouths.

So I walk out there in my crappy jeans and T-shirt. The crowd cheers as loud for me as they did for the actors. I see Dad in the middle of the theater. He's grinning and clapping harder than anyone.

I finally smile and bow. You know what? This feels pretty damn good.

WANT TO KEEP READING?

Turn the page for a sneak peek at another book from the Gravel Road Rural series: M.G. Higgins's *Rodeo Princess*.

ISBN: 978-1-68021-061-3

Chapter 1

Freddie tosses his head. Prances. I know he'd like to go full out. I pat his neck. "Not now, boy. Barrel drills tomorrow. I promise."

Today, it's endurance. Building his stamina. The goal is Evans Lake. Thirty miles round trip.

The wind picks up behind me. Goes right through my fleece jacket. I twist in the saddle. Dark clouds are building. Another storm? It's late April. This Montana winter is lasting forever. I squeeze my legs. Urge Freddie to a brisk walk. His hooves splatter through muddy snowmelt.

We get to Rattlesnake Hill. It borders the McNair ranch. I could go around it. But I pull Freddie to a stop. Take a moment to decide. Realize the decision was made when I came this way in the first place.

I turn his head toward the narrow cattle trail. I don't have to ask. He takes it at a trot. Zigzags to the top. He's so loyal. Such a willing accomplice. We get to the peak. He's breathing hard. So am I. But not from exertion.

Below us lies the McNair ranch. Two-story log cabin mansion. Stable bigger than our double-wide trailer. Covered riding arena. Fenced and cross-fenced pastures. About fifty quarter horses that I can see. Someone is lunging a palomino in an outdoor arena. Too far away to tell exactly who it is. Too short and thin for Mr. McNair. Probably one of his hands. Or a new trainer. They're always hiring new trainers. The ones raved about in horse magazines.

I'm about to pull Freddie around when I see movement. Under the roof of the covered arena. Horse's legs. Red boots. A smooth canter. Could be Amy McNair. Or her mom. Or one of Amy's friends. She's quickly out of sight again. I could wait for another glance. Decide against it. I'm not that desperate.

I click my tongue. Freddie scurries down the hill. We're soon back on the trail. To hell with taking it easy. I loosen the reins. Give him his head. The wind whips my face. We sprint a good ways. I slow him down. Ask myself if that glimpse of my former life was worth it. I don't feel any better for it. So, no. It wasn't.

We get to Evans Lake. The clouds are almost overhead now. Dark. Stormy. Snow in them, for sure. The temperature has dropped several more degrees. Damn. I could have sworn it was spring this morning. I should have checked the weather report. It was stupid of me not to.

I turn Freddie. Fifteen miles to home. I don't want to

push him. But I have to. I'm not dressed for snow. He willingly speeds up. He wants to get to his oat bucket as much as I want him there.

Bits of falling ice prick my face. Then thick, wet flakes. I urge Freddie to a gallop.

Halfway home and it's a full-on blizzard. Can't see more than a few feet ahead. I tug the reins. Just as I do, Freddie trips. Goes down on a knee. I barely stay in the saddle. Right away he's up again. Walking. I should stop him. Check his legs. But he's not limping. And I'm really cold. Too cold. I didn't even think to bring gloves.

I pull my hat down tight. Wrap the reins around the saddle horn. Slip my hands under my arms to keep them warm. Let Freddie use his instincts. Guide us home.

I can just make out our stable's blue roof. I'm shivering. My teeth are chattering. I slide off. Lead Freddie inside. Quickly take off his saddle and bridle. Make sure he has water and hay. I'll have to brush him later. I need to get inside. Need to get warm.

We never heat the double-wide more than sixty-five degrees to save money. But the kitchen feels blessedly warm compared to outside. I rush to my bedroom. Change out of my wet clothes. Throw on a jacket. Wrap a blanket around my shoulders. I'm still shivering. Back in the kitchen I make a pot of coffee. Sit at the table. Hunch my shoulders. Clasp the hot mug between my palms.

The house is empty. Is it possible my dad and brothers are out looking for me? No. I left early this morning. None of them was up yet. I didn't leave a note. They wouldn't have known where I was.

I look out the window. The snow has stopped. I should get back to the stable. Take care of Freddie and the other horses. But the cold has seeped deep into my bones. I feel frozen. Like I'll never move again.

The door bangs open. Dad barges in. Followed by my two older brothers. They wipe their muddy boots on the mat. Toss their coats onto the hooks near the door. They fill the kitchen.

"Where were you off to this morning?" Dad asks.

"Gave Freddie a ride," I answer.

He grabs a beer from the fridge. "Did you get stuck in that storm?"

"Yeah."

"That came out of nowhere. You okay?"

"Just cold. Where were you?" I ask.

"In town."

My brothers grab beers too. "Hey, what's for dinner?" Toby asks me.

I glance at the clock. Can't believe it's five already. "I don't know." I shrug the blanket off my shoulders. Nothing warms me up like the male members of my family. They're better than a furnace.

"Soon, okay?" Seth says. "We're going out again."

They disappear down the hall. I set my coffee cup on the table. Stare at it a second longer. Pull myself up. Search through cupboards. Find canned stew in the pantry. Heat it on the stove. Peel a few carrots. Toss a box of crackers on the counter. Dinner is fixed in ten minutes. They're done eating it ten minutes later.

Toby and Seth stride to the back door.

"You're leaving *now*?" I say. "What about Mom?"

They glance at each other. Shrug their shoulders. Seth says, "Tell her hi for us."

"Tell her yourself! You can't wait a few minutes?" Then I see Dad is joining them. "You too?" I say.

"We're going to the basketball game. Garth's son is playing. Saw him in town. Promised we'd go. Cheer for his kid." He runs his hand over his bald head. "Tell her … I miss her. Okay?"

They're out the door. The kitchen is empty again. The temperature drops a few degrees.

ABOUT THE AUTHOR

M.G. Higgins writes fiction and nonfiction for children and young adults.

Her novel *Bi-Normal* won the 2013 Independent Publisher (IPPY) silver medal for Young Adult Fiction. Her novel *Falling Out of Place* was a 2013 Next Generation Indie Book Awards finalist and a 2014 Young Adult Library Services Association (YALSA) Quick Pick nominee. Her novel *I'm Just Me* won the 2014 IPPY silver medal for Multicultural Fiction—Juvenile/Young Adult. It was also a YALSA Quick Pick nominee.

Ms. Higgins's nearly thirty nonfiction titles range from science and technology to history and biographies. While her wide range of topics reflects her varied interests, she especially enjoys writing about mental health issues.

Before becoming a full-time writer, she worked as a school counselor and had a private counseling practice.

When she's not writing, Ms. Higgins enjoys hiking and taking photographs in the Arizona desert where she lives with her husband.